WHO KILLED
THE MYSTERIOUS LADY
IN LILAC?

She was always dressed in mauve, and always alone. Staring straight before her, she registered, but never acknowledged, the admiring glances of passers-by.

Even before her murder, she aroused the sleuth in Maigret. As the Inspector and his wife took the sulphurous spring waters of Vichy, they speculated. What past adventures surrounded the quiet lady in lilac?

But suddenly, she was found strangled. Papers, clothing, jewelry were scattered all around her comfortable home, but seemingly nothing of value was missing.

Now, for Maigret, the sleuthing would begin in earnest . . .

"EVERY SIMENON NOVEL IS A PURE DE-LIGHT if only because there are few craftsmen of his ability and perception . . . MAIGRET IN VICHY is a particularly good example of the purity and intensity of Simenon's awareness of how people live. Don't miss it."

Book-of-the-Month Club News

"HIS WORK COMBINES GREATER REWARDS WITH FEWER DEMANDS than that of any writer I know. He frequently gives us something that lies very close to the heart of art. In his chronicles of Inspector Maigret, the special virtues are a careful, intuitive psychological unraveling and the reassuring, normative, undemonstratively life-affirming presence of Maigret himself."

Washington Post

Avon Classic Crime Collection

Charlotte Jay
BEAT NOT THE BONE

Cornelius Hirschberg
FLORENTINE FINIS!

Mary Kelly
DEAD CORSE

Dorothy B. Hughes
THE EXPENDABLE MAN

Dick Francis
DEAD CERT

Patrick Quentin
PUZZLE FOR FOOLS

Hilda Lawrence
DEATH OF A DOLL

W. Somerset Maugham
ASHENDEN

Vera Caspary
LAURA

Rex Stout
WHERE THERE'S A WILL

Henry Maxfield
LEGACY OF A SPY

E. C. Bentley
TRENT'S LAST CASE

Philip MacDonald
THE RASP

Michael Innes
ONE MAN SHOW

Robert Van Gulik
THE CHINESE BELL MURDER:

C. P. Snow
DEATH UNDER SAIL

John Dickson Carr

MAIGRET IN VICHY

Georges Simenon

Translated from the French
by Eileen Ellenbogen

A Helen and Kurt Wolff Book

AVON
CLASSIC CRIME
COLLECTION

AVON BOOKS
A division of
The Hearst Corporation
959 Eighth Avenue
New York, New York 10019

ISBN: 0-380-00510-7

First Avon Printing, October, 1970
Third Printing, October, 1975

Printed in the U.S.A.

1

"Do you know them?" Madame Maigret asked in an undertone, observing that her husband was looking back over his shoulder at the couple who had just gone past.

The man, too, had turned his head and was smiling. He seemed hesitant, as though considering retracing his steps to shake the Chief Superintendent by the hand.

"No, I don't think so. . . . I don't know. . . ."

He was a squat little man. His wife, too, was small and plump, though perhaps an inch or so taller. Why was it Maigret had the impression that she was a Belgian? Because of her fair skin, her hair that was almost buttercup yellow, her protuberant blue eyes?

This was their fifth or sixth encounter. The first time, the man had stopped dead, beaming in delighted surprise. He had stood there uncertainly, as if about to speak, while the Chief Superintendent, frowning, searched his memory in vain.

There was certainly something familiar about that face and figure, but what the devil was it?

Where had he last seen this cheerful little man, with the wife who looked as though she were made of brightly colored marzipan?

"I really can't think. . . ."

It did not much matter. Besides, everybody here was different from the people one met in everyday life. Any minute, now, there would be a burst of music. On the bandstand, with its slender columns and ornate canopy, the uniformed bandsmen, their eyes fixed on the conductor, sat waiting to raise the brass instruments to their lips. This presumably was the Municipal Band, made up of firemen and other Council workers. Their uniform was splendid, with scarlet tabs, white sashes, and enough gold braid and embroidery to satisfy a South American General.

Hundreds—thousands, it seemed to him—of iron chairs done up with yellow paint were set out in concentric circles around the bandstand, and nearly all were occupied by silent, waiting men and women with solemn faces.

In a minute or two, at nine o'clock, amid the great trees of the park, the concert would begin. After an oppressively hot day, the evening air seemed almost cool, and a light breeze rustled the leaves. Here and there, lamp standards surmounted by milky globes lightened the dark foliage with patches of paler green.

"Do you want to sit?"

There were still a few empty chairs, but they did not avail themselves of them. This evening, as always, they preferred to walk about in a leisurely way. Other couples, like themselves, came and went, half listening to the music, but there was also a number of solitary men and women, almost all elderly.

Nothing seemed quite real somehow. The white casino, plastered with the ornate moldings so much in vogue at the turn of the century, was floodlit. Except for the occasional blare of a motor horn in Rue Georges-Clemenceau, one could almost believe that here time stood still.

"There she is..." whispered Madame Maigret, pointing with her chin.

It had become a sort of game. She had got into the habit of following her husband's glance, watching for any glimmer of surprise or interest.

What else was there for them to do with their time? They walked, or rather strolled, about the streets. From time to time they paused, not because they were out of breath, but to look more closely at the play of light on a tree, a house, or a face.

They felt as though they had been in Vichy since the dawn of time, although, in fact, this was only their fifth day. Already they had established a routine, to which they adhered rigorously, as though it really mattered, and their days were given up to a succession of rituals, which they performed with the utmost solemnity.

How seriously, in fact, did Maigret take it all? His wife sometimes wondered, stealing a covert glance at him, trying to read his mind. He was not the man he was in Paris. His walk was less brisk, his features were less drawn. He went about most of the time smiling but abstracted. His expression suggested a degree of satisfaction, certainly, but also, perhaps, a touch of sardonic self-mockery.

"She's wearing her white shawl."

Each new day found them in the same place at the same hour, in one of the shaded park walks, beside the Allier, on a boulevard lined with plane trees, or in a crowded or a deserted side street, and, because of this, they had come to recognize, here and there, a face or a figure, and these were already getting to be part of their world.

Was it not the case that everyone here was going through the same motions at the same time every hour of the day, and not just at the mineral springs, where they all forgathered for the hallowed glass of water?

Maigret's eyes rested on a figure in the crowd, and sharpened. His wife followed his glance.

"Is she a widow, do you think?"

They might well have christened her "the lady in mauve," or rather "the lady in lilac," because that was the color she always wore. Tonight she must has arrived late, because she was sitting in one of the back rows.

The previous evening, at about eight o'clock, the Maigrets had come upon her unexpectedly as they were walking past the bandstand. There was still an hour to go before the concert. The little yellow chairs were so neatly arranged in concentric rings that they might have been circles drawn with a compass. All the chairs were vacant except one, in the front row, where the lady in lilac was sitting. There was something pathetic about her. She did not attempt to read by the light of the nearby lamp. She was not knitting. She was not doing anything. She did not seem in the least restless. She sat motionless, very upright, with her hands lying flat in her lap, looking straight in front of her, like a public figure avoiding the stares of the crowd.

She could have come straight out of a picture book. Unlike most of the women here, who went about bareheaded, she wore a white hat. The filmy shawl draped over her shoulders was white too. Her dress was of that distinctive lilac color that she seemed so much attached to.

She had an unusually long, narrow face and thin lips.

"She must be an old maid, don't you think?"

Maigret was unwilling to commit himself. He was not conducting an inquiry or following a trail. Here he was under no obligation to study people's faces, hoping that they would reveal the truth about themselves.

All the same, every now and then he caught himself doing it. He could not help it. It had become second nature. For no reason at all, he would find himself taking an interest in someone in the crowd, trying to guess his occupation, his domestic circumstances, the kind of life he led when he was not taking the waters.

It was by no means easy. After the first few days, sometimes after the first few hours, everyone seemed to become assimilated. Almost all wore the same expression of slightly vacant serenity, except those who were seriously ill, and who stood out from the rest by virtue of their deformities, their painful movements, and, still more, the unmistakable look in their eyes of pain tempered with hope.

The lady in lilac was one of what might be

described as Maigret's circle of intimates, one of those who had attracted his attention and intrigued him from the first.

It was hard to guess her age. She might be forty-five or fifty-five. Time had not imprinted any telltale lines on her face.

She gave the impression of a woman accustomed to silence, like a nun, used to solitude, even perhaps enjoying it. Whether walking or, as at present, sitting, she totally ignored the people around her. No doubt it would have surprised her to know that Chief Superintendent Maigret, not as a matter of professional duty but simply for his own satisfaction, was studying her, in the hope of finding out what she was really like.

"She's never lived with a man, I'd say," he replied, as the opening burst of music came from the bandstand.

"Nor with children. Perhaps with someone very old, though. She might, perhaps, have had an aged mother to look after."

If so, she was unlikely to have been a good nurse, since she appeared unbending and unsociable. If she failed to see the people around her, it was because she did not look at them. She looked inward. She looked within herself, seeing no one but herself, deriving, no doubt, some secret satisfaction from this self-absorption.

"Shall we go?"

They had not come to listen to the music. They had simply got into the habit of walking past the bandstand at this time of the evening. Besides, it was not every night that there was a concert. Some evenings, it was virtually deserted on this side of the park. They strolled across the park, turning right into the colonnade which ran beside a street brilliant with neon signs. They could see hotels, restaurants, shops, a cinema. They had not yet been to the cinema. It did not fit in with their timetable.

There were other people taking a walk like themselves, at more or less the same leisurely pace, some coming, some going. A few had cut short their walk to go to the casino theater. They were late, and could be seen hurrying in, one or two here and there in evening dress.

Every one of these people lived quite a different life somewhere else, in a district of Paris, in some little provincial town, in Brussels, Amsterdam, Rome, or Philadelphia.

Each was a part of some predetermined social order, with its own rules, taboos, and passwords. Some were rich, others poor. Some were so ill that the treatment could do no more than give them a little extra time: others felt that, after taking the cure, they could forget about their health for the rest of the year.

This place was a kind of melting pot. Maigret's own case was typical. It had all started one evening when they were dining with the Pardons. Madame Pardon had served *canard au sang*, a dish that she made to perfection, and which the Chief Superintendent particularly relished.

"Is there anything wrong with it?" she had asked anxiously, seeing that Maigret had barely tasted it.

Surprised, Pardon had turned to his guest and

11

subjected him to a searching look. Then, sounding really worried, he had asked:

"Aren't you feeling well?"

"Just a twinge . . . It's nothing. . . ."

The doctor, however, had not failed to notice his friend's unwonted pallor, and the beads of perspiration on his forehead.

The subject was not mentioned again during dinner. The Chief Superintendent had scarcely touched his wine, and when, over coffee, he was offered a glass of old Armagnac, he had waved it away:

"Not tonight, if you don't mind."

It was not until some time later that Doctor Pardon had said quietly:

"Let's go into my consulting room, shall we?"

Maigret had agreed reluctantly. He had known for some time that this was bound to happen, but he had kept putting it off from one day to the next. Doctor Pardon's consulting room was small and by no means luxurious. His stethoscope lay on the desk amid a litter of bottles, jars, and papers, and the couch on which he examined his patients sagged in the middle, as though the last one had left the imprint of his body on it.

"What seems to be the trouble, Maigret?"

"I don't know. It's my age, I daresay."

"How old are you? Fifty-two?"

"Fifty-three. . . . I've had a lot on my hands lately. Work . . . Worry . . . No sensational cases . . . Nothing exciting . . . Just the opposite . . . On the one hand, a flood of paperwork arising out of the reorganization at the Law Courts. . . . On the other, an epidemic of assaults on young girls

12

and women living alone, in some cases including rape, in some not. . . . The press is howling for blood, and I haven't the staff to put on full-scale patrols without disrupting my whole department. . . ."

"Do you suffer from indigestion?"

"I do occasionally have stomach cramps . . . pains . . . as I did tonight . . . or rather a kind of constriction in the chest and abdomen. . . . I feel leaden . . . tired."

"Would you mind if I had a look at you?"

His wife, in the next room, must have guessed, Madame Pardon too, and this bothered Maigret. He had a horror of anything to do with illness.

As he stripped off his tie, jacket, shirt, and undershirt, he recalled something he had said when he was still in his teens: "I'd rather die young than live the life of an invalid, all pills and potions and diets, and being made to do this and not being allowed to do that."

In his vocabulary, being an invalid meant listening to one's heart, worrying about one's stomach, liver, and kidneys, and, at more or less regular intervals, exposing one's naked body to a doctor.

He no longer talked glibly of dying young, but he still did not feel ready to enter the invalid state.

"My trousers too?"

"Just pull them down a little."

Pardon took his blood pressure, listened to his chest, felt his diaphragm and stomach, pressing here and there with a finger.

"Am I hurting you?"

"No. . . . A little tenderness there, I think. . . . No . . . lower down. . . ."

Well, here he was, behaving just like anyone else, apprehensive, ashamed of his own cowardice, afraid to look his old friend in the face. Awkwardly, he began putting on his clothes again. When Pardon spoke, there was no change in his voice:

"When did you last take a holiday?"

"Last year I managed to get away for a week, then I was recalled because . . ."

"What about the year before last?"

"I couldn't leave Paris."

"Considering the life you lead, you ought to be in very much worse shape than you are."

"What about my liver?"

"It has stood up valiantly, considering the way you've treated it. . . . Admittedly, it's slightly enlarged, but it's in excellent working order."

"What's wrong, then?"

"There's nothing precisely wrong. . . . A little of everything. . . . How do you feel when you wake up in the morning?"

"Like a bear with a sore head."

Pardon laughed.

"Do you sleep well?"

"According to my wife, I thrash about in bed, and occasionally talk in my sleep."

"I see you're not smoking."

"I'm trying to cut down on it."

"Why?"

"I don't know. . . . I'm trying to cut down on drink, too."

"Sit down, won't you?"

14

Pardon sat in the chair behind his desk. Here, in his consulting room, he was very much the medical man, quite different from the host entertaining in his drawing room or dining room.

"Just you listen to me. You're not ill. As a matter of fact, considering your age and the life you lead, you're quite remarkably fit. I'll thank you to get that into your head once and for all. Stop fretting about every little twinge and odd pain here and there, and don't start worrying every time you go up a flight of stairs. . . ."

"How did you know?"

"Tell me, when you're questioning a suspect, how do *you* know?"

They were both smiling.

"Here we are in June. Paris is sweltering. You'll oblige me by taking a holiday at once, if possible leaving no forwarding address. . . . At any rate, I'm sure you'll have the good sense not to call up the Quai des Orfèvres every day. . . ."

"I daresay it could be managed," Maigret said, not very graciously. "There's our cottage at Meung-sur-Loire. . . ."

"You'll have plenty of time to enjoy that when you retire. . . . This year, I have other plans for you. . . . Do you know Vichy at all?"

"I've never set foot in the place, in spite of the fact that I was born within forty miles of it, near Moulins. . . . But in those days, of course, not everyone owned a car. . . ."

"That reminds me, has your wife passed her test?"

"We've actually got as far as buying a small car."

"I don't think you could do better than take the waters at Vichy. It will do you a world of good. ... A thorough clean-out of the system. ..."

When he saw the look on the Chief Superintendent's face, he almost burst out laughing.

"You want me to take the cure?"

"It will only mean drinking a few pints of water every day. ... I don't suppose the specialist will insist on your having all the trimmings: mud baths, mineral baths, vibro-massage, and all that nonsense. There's nothing seriously wrong with you. Three weeks of rest and regular exercise, no worry ..."

"No beer, no wine, nothing to eat but rabbit's food ..."

"You've had a good many years of eating and drinking whatever you fancied, haven't you?"

"That's true," he had to admit.

"And you have many more ahead, even if you do have to be a little more moderate in the future. ... Are we agreed, then?"

Maigret got to his feet and, much to his own astonishment, heard himself saying, just as though he were any other patient of Pardon's:

"Agreed."

"When will you go?"

"In a day or two, a week at the outside. Just long enough to catch up with my paper work."

"I'll have to hand you over to a man on the spot who will be able to tell you more than I can. ... I could name half a dozen. Let me think. ... There's Rian, a decent young fellow, not too full of himself. ... I'll give you his address and telephone number. And I'll drop him a line tomorrow, to put him in the picture. . . ."

"I'm much obliged, Pardon."

"I wasn't too rough with you, I hope?"

"You couldn't have been more gentle."

Returning to the drawing room, he smiled at his wife, a reassuring smile. But nothing was said, illness not being considered a suitable topic for after-dinner conversation at the Pardons'.

It was not until they reached Rue Popincourt, walking arm in arm, that Maigret remarked casually, as though it were a matter of no importance:

"We're going to Vichy for our holiday."

"Will you be taking the cure?"

"I suppose I might as well while I'm there!" he said wryly. "There's nothing wrong with me. In fact, I gather I'm exceptionally healthy, which is why I'm being packed off to take the waters, I daresay!"

That evening at the Pardons' had not really been the start of it. He had for some time been obsessed by the strange notion that everybody was younger than he was, from the Chief Commissioner and the examining magistrates to the prisoners brought in for questioning. And now there was Doctor Rian, fair-haired and affable, and well on the right side of forty.

A kid, in other words, at any rate a young man, but none the less sober and self-assured for all that. And this was the man who was to be the arbiter of his, Chief Superintendent Maigret's, fate. Well, more or less. . . .

Maigret was irritated and at the same time apprehensive, for he certainly did not feel old, nor even middle-aged.

For all his youth, Doctor Rian lived in an elegant red-brick house in Boulevard des Etats-Unis. Maybe it was rather too Edwardian in style, but it had a certain grandeur, with its marble staircase, its handsome carpets, its highly polished furniture. There was even a maid in a lace-trimmed cap.

"I presume your parents are dead? What did your father die of?"

The doctor carefully wrote down his answers on a memo pad, in a neat, clerical hand.

"And your mother? ... Any brothers? ... Sisters? ... Childhood ailments? ... Measles? ... Chicken pox? ..."

Chicken pox no, measles yes, when he was very small and his mother was still living. It was, in fact, his warmest and most vivid memory of his mother, who died very shortly afterward.

"How about games and sport? ... Have you ever had an accident? ... Are you subject to sore throats? ... You're a heavy smoker, I take it? ..."

The young doctor smiled, with a touch of mischief, by way of showing Maigret that he knew him by repute.

"No one could say that you lead a sedentary life, exactly."

"It varies. Sometimes I don't set foot outside my office for two or three weeks at a time, and then, all of a sudden, I'm running around all over the place for days on end."

"Regular meals?"

"No."

"Do you watch your diet?"

He was forced to admit that he liked rich food, especially highly seasoned stews and sauces.

"Not just a gourmet, in fact, but a hearty eater?"

"You could say so, yes."

"What about wine? A half-bottle, a bottle a day?"

"Yes ... No ... More ... As a rule I don't have more than two or three glasses with my dinner. .... Occasionally I have a beer sent up to the office from the brasserie nearby."

"Spirits?"

"I quite often have an apéritif with a colleague."

In the Brasserie Dauphine. It wasn't the drink itself but the clubbable atmosphere, the cooking smells, the aroma of aniseed and Calvados, with which, by this time, the very walls were impregnated. Why should he feel ashamed, all of a sudden, in the presence of this neat, well-set-up young man in his luxurious consulting room?

"In other words, you don't drink to excess?"

He had no wish to conceal anything.

"It depends on what you mean by excess. I'm not averse to a glass or two of sloe gin after dinner. My sister-in-law sends it from Alsace. .... And then often, when I'm working on a case, I'm in and out of cafés and bars a great deal. .... How shall I put it? If, at the start of a case, I happen to be in a bistro where Vouvray is a specialty, as likely as not I'll go on drinking Vouvray right through to the end."

"How much in a day?"

It reminded him of his boyhood, the confessional in the village church, smelling of mildew and the curé's snuff.

"A lot?"

"It would seem a lot to you, I daresay."

"For how long at a stretch?"

"Anything from three to ten days, sometimes even longer. It's a matter of chance. . . ."

There were no reproaches, no penances, but he had a pretty shrewd idea what the doctor thought of him, as he sat, elbows on his handsome mahogany desk, with the sun shining on his fair hair.

"No severe indigestion? No heartburn or giddiness?"

Giddiness, yes. Nothing serious. From time to time, especially of late, the ground seemed to tilt slightly, and everything about him appeared a little unreal. He felt off balance, unsteady on his feet.

It was not bad enough to cause him any serious anxiety, but it was an unpleasant sensation. Fortunately, it never lasted more than a couple of minutes. On one occasion, he had just left the Law Courts and was about to cross the road. He had waited until it was over, before venturing to step off the pavement.

"I see . . . I see."

What did he see? That he was a sick man? That he smoked heavily and drank too much? That it was high time, at his age, that he learned to watch his diet?

Maigret was not letting it get him down. He smiled in the way his wife had grown used to, since they had come to Vichy. It was a self-mocking smile, if a little morose.

"Come with me, please."

This time he was given the full treatment. He was made to climb up and down a ladder repeatedly for three full minutes. He had his blood pressure taken lying down, sitting up, and standing. Then he was X-rayed.

"Breathe in . . . Deeper . . . Hold it . . . Breathe out . . . In . . . Hold it . . . Out . . ."

It was comical yet somehow distressing, dramatic and at the same time slightly dotty. He had, perhaps, thirty years of life still to look forward to, and yet any minute now he might be tactfully informed that his life as a healthy, active man was over, and that henceforth he would be reduced to the status of an invalid.

They had all been through this experience, all the people one saw in the park, under the spreading trees, at the mineral springs, on the lake shore. Even the members of the Sporting Club across the river, whom one could watch sunbathing, or playing tennis or bowls in the shade, had been through it.

"Mademoiselle Jeanne."

"Yes, sir."

The receptionist knew what was wanted. It was all part of a familiar routine. Soon the Maigrets would be following a routine of their own.

First, the little needle or the prick on the finger tip, then the glass slides and phials for the blood smears.

"Relax. . . . Clench your fist."

He felt the prick of a needle in the crook of his elbow.

"Right, that will do."

21

He had had blood samples taken before, but this time, it seemed to him, there was something portentous about it.

"Thank you. You can get dressed now."

A few minutes later they were back in the consulting room, with its walls lined with books and bound volumes of medical journals.

"I don't think any very drastic treatment is needed in your case. Come and see me again at this time the day after tomorrow. By then I shall have the results of the tests. Meanwhile, I'm going to put you on a diet. I presume you're staying in a hotel? Here is a diet sheet. All you have to do is to hand it to the headwaiter. He'll attend to it."

It was a card with forbidden foods printed in one column and permitted ones in the other. It even went so far as to list sample menus on the back.

"I don't know if you are aware of the different chemical properties of the various springs. There is an excellent little handbook on the subject, written by one of my colleagues, but it may be out of print. For a start, I want you to alternate between two springs, Chomel and Grande Grille. You'll find them both in the park."

Both men looked equally solemn. Maigret felt not the least inclination, as he watched the doctor scribbling notes on his pad, to shrug the whole thing off, or indulge in a little secret smile.

"Do you usually have an early breakfast? I see. . . . Is your wife here with you? . . . In that case, I don't want to send you halfway across town on an empty stomach. Let's see. You'd better start at about ten thirty in the morning at the

Grande Grille. There are plenty of chairs, so you won't have to stand about, and if it rains there's a huge glass enclosure for shelter. . . . I want you to have three half-pints of water at half-hourly intervals, and it should be drunk as hot as you can take it.

"I want you to repeat the process in the afternoons at about five, at the Chomel spring.

"Don't worry if you feel a bit languid the first day. It's a purely temporary side effect of the treatment. . . . Anyway, I shall be seeing you. . . ."

Those early days, before his initiation into the mysteries of each individual spring, seemed very far away now. Now, as for thousands of others, as for tens of thousands of others, with whom he rubbed shoulders every hour of the day, the cure had become a part of his life.

Just as in the evening, when there was a concert, every one of the little yellow chairs around the bandstand was occupied, so, at certain times of day, there was not a chair to be had, so great was the crowd gathered around the springs, all waiting for a second, third, or fourth glass of the waters.

Like everyone else, they had brought measuring glasses, Madame Maigret having insisted on getting one for herself.

"But *you're* not taking the waters!"

"Why shouldn't I? Where's the harm? It says in one of the pamphlets that the waters are slimming. . . ."

Each glass had its own case of plaited straw, and Madame Maigret carried both of theirs slung over one shoulder like binoculars at a race meeting.

They had never walked so much in their lives. Their hotel was in the France district, a quiet part of the town near the Célestins spring. They were out and about by nine every morning, when, apart from the delivery man, they had the streets almost to themselves.

A few minutes' walk from their hotel there was a children's playground with a' wading pool, swings, play apparatus of all sorts, even a puppet theater, more elaborate than the one in the Champs-Elysées.

"Your tickets, sir?"

They had bought two one-franc tickets, and strolled among the trees, watching the half-naked children at play. Next day they had come again.

"We sell books of twenty tickets at a reduced rate."

They were reluctant to commit themselves so far ahead. They had come upon the playground by chance and, for want of anything better to do, had fallen into the habit of returning there every day at the same hour.

Regularly, they went on from there to the bowling club, where they would watch two or three games being played, with Maigret attentively following every throw, especially those of the tall, thin, one-armed man, always to be found under the same tree, who was, in spite of his disability, the finest player of all. Another regular player was a dignified old gentleman with pink cheeks, snow-white hair, and a southern accent, always addressed by his companions as "Senator."

It was not far from there to the lifeguards' station and the beach, with buoys bobbing in the water to mark the limits of the bathing area. Here, too, they would find the same familiar faces under the same familiar beach umbrellas.

"You're not bored, are you?" she had asked him on their second day.

"Why on earth should I be?" he had retorted in surprise.

For indeed he was not bored. Little by little his habits, his tempo of living, were changing. For instance, he caught himself filling his pipe on the Pont de Bellerive and realized, to his amazement, that he always smoked a pipe just at this time and place. There was also the Yacht Club pipe, which he smoked while watching the young people skimming over the water on skis.

"It's a dangerous sport, wouldn't you say?"

"In what way?"

Finally the park, the attendant filling their glasses from the spring, the two of them drinking the water in little sips. It was hot and salty. The water from the Chomel spring tasted strongly of sulphur, and after drinking it Maigret could hardly wait to light his pipe.

It amazed Madame Maigret that he should take it all so calmly. It was most unlike him to be so docile. It quite worried her at times, until it dawned on her that he was amusing himself by playing at detection. Almost in spite of himself he watched people, classifying them, taking note of everything about them, down to the smallest detail. He had, for instance, already discovered which of their fellow guests in the Hôtel de la

Bérézina—more a family pension than a hotel—had liver trouble and which diabetes, simply by observing what they had to eat.

What was this one's life history? What did that one do for a living? These were his preoccupations, in which he sometimes invited his wife to share.

Especially intriguing to them were the couple whom they called "the happy pair," the dumpy little man who seemed always on the verge of coming up to shake his hand, and his diminutive wife who looked like something out of a confectioner's shop. What was their station in life? They seemed to recognize the Chief Superintendent, but was this not perhaps merely because they had seen his picture in the papers?

Not many people here did, in fact, recognize him, many fewer than in Paris. Admittedly, his wife had insisted on buying him a light mohair jacket, almost white in fact, of the kind that elderly men used to wear when he was a boy. But even allowing for this, it would probably not have occurred to most people that the head of the Paris C.I.D. could be here, in Vichy. When anyone peered at him with a puzzled frown, or turned back to look at him, he felt sure that they were thinking:

"Good heavens! That might almost be Maigret!"

But they did not think that it *was* Maigret. And no wonder. He scarcely recognized himself!

Another person who intrigued them was the lady in lilac. She too was taking the waters, but only at the Grande Grille, where she could be seen every morning. She always sat a little removed from the crowd, near the newspaper stand. She never drank more than a mouthful of the water. Afterward, with her usual air of remote dignity, she would rinse out her glass, and put it away carefully in its straw case.

There were usually one or two people in the crowd who seemed to know her well enough to greet her. The Maigrets never saw her in the afternoon. Was she perhaps undergoing hydrotherapy? Or had she been ordered by her doctor to take an afternoon rest?

Doctor Rian had said:

"E.R.S., perfect. Average sed rate: 6 mm. per hour. . . . Cholesterol, a little on the high side, but well within the normal range. . . . Urea normal. . . . You're a bit low on iron, but there's no cause for anxiety. . . . No need to worry about uric acid, either . . . just keep off game, shellfish, and variety meats. As to your blood count, it could scarcely be better, with 98 per cent hemoglobin.

"There's nothing wrong with you that a thorough clean-out won't cure. . . . Any headaches or unusual fatigue? . . . Right, then, we'll keep on with the same treatment and diet for the next few days. . . . Come and see me again on Saturday."

There was an open-air band concert that night. They did not see the lady in lilac leave, because, as usual, they themselves left early, well before the end. The Hôtel de la Bérézina, in the France district of the town, gleamed with fresh paint, and its double doors were flanked on either side by flowering shrubs in urns. The Maigrets enjoyed walking back to it through the deserted streets.

They slept in a brass bed, and all the furniture in their room was in the style of the early 1900s— like the bath, which was raised on legs, and had old-fashioned goose-neck taps.

The hotel was well kept and very quiet, except when the Gagnaire boys, who had rooms on the first floor, were let loose in the garden to play at cowboys and Indians.

Everyone was asleep.

Was it the fifth day? Or the sixth? Of the two, it was Madame Maigret who was the more confused, waking up as she did every morning to the realization that she need not get up to make the coffee. Their breakfast was brought in on a tray at seven o'clock, coffee and fresh croissants, and the *Journal de Clermont-Ferrand*, which devoted two pages to news and features about life in Vichy.

Maigret had got into the habit of reading the paper from cover to cover, so that by now there was precious little he did not know about local affairs. He even read the obituaries and the small ads.

"Desirable residence, in excellent repair. Three rooms, bathroom, all mod. cons. Uninterrupted view . . ."

"Are you thinking of buying a house?"

"No, but this is interesting. I can't help wondering who will buy it. A family coming regularly for the cure, who won't live in it for more than a month each year? An elderly couple from Paris who want to retire here? Or . . ."

They got dressed, taking turns in the bathroom,

28

and went down the staircase, with its red carpet held in place by triangular brass clips. The proprietor was there in the hall, always ready with a friendly greeting. He was not a local man, as was obvious from his accent, but came from Montélimar.

They nibbled the hours away. The children's playground . . . The bowling greens . . .

"I see, by the way, that Wednesdays and Saturdays are market days. It's a big market. We might go and have a look around. . . ."

They had always been attracted to markets, their stalls laden with sides of beef, fish, and live lobsters, and their all-pervading smell of fresh fruit and vegetables.

"Well, Rian did advise me to walk four miles a day," he remarked with heavy irony, adding:

"Little does he know that, on the average, we cover the best part of twelve!"

"Do you really think so?"

"Work it out. We spend at least five hours a day walking. . . . We may not be striding out like a couple of athletes, but all the same we can't be doing much less than three miles an hour."

"I'd never have thought it!"

The glass of water. Sitting on one of the yellow chairs, reading the papers that had just come from Paris. Lunch in the white dining room, where the only touch of color was an opened bottle of wine on a table here and there, labeled with the name of the resident who had ordered it. There was no wine on the Maigrets' table.

"Did he say no wine?"

"Not in so many words. But while I'm about it..."

She could not get over the fact that, while scrupulously keeping to his diet, he was, at the same time, perfectly good-tempered about it.

They permitted themselves a short rest after lunch, before setting off again, this time for the opposite end of the town. Here, where most of the shops were, the pavements were so crowded that they were seldom able to walk abreast.

"Was there ever a town with so many osteopaths and chiropodists!"

"It's no wonder, if everyone walks as much as we do!"

That evening the bandstand in the park was deserted. Instead, there was a concert in the gardens of the Grand Casino. Here, in place of the brass band, a string orchestra played. The music was of a more serious kind, matched by the expressions on the faces of the audience.

They did not see the lady in lilac. They had not seen her in the park either, though they had caught a glimpse of "the happy pair," who tonight were more formally dressed than usual, and seemed to be going to the casino theater, where a light comedy was playing.

The brass bedstead. It was astonishing how quickly the days went by, even when one was doing absolutely nothing. Croissants, coffee, cubes of sugar in greaseproof wrappings, the *Journal de Clermont-Ferrand*.

Maigret, in pajamas, was sitting in an armchair next to the window, smoking his first pipe of the day. His coffee cup was still half full. He enjoyed lingering over it as long as possible.

His sudden exclamation brought Madame Maigret from the bathroom, in a blue flower-printed dressing gown, with her toothbrush still in her hand.

"What's the matter?"

"Look at this."

There, on the first page devoted to Vichy, was a photograph, a photograph of the lady in lilac. It was not a very recent one. She looked several years younger in it and, for the occasion, had managed to produce a tight-lipped semblance of a smile.

"What's happened to her?"

"She's been murdered."

"Last night?"

"If it had happened last night, it wouldn't be in this morning's paper. No, it was the night before."

"But we saw her at the band concert."

"Yes, at nine o'clock. . . . She lived only a couple of streets from here, Rue du Bourbonnais. . . . I had a feeling that we were almost neighbors. . . . She went home. . . . She had time to take off her shawl and hat and go into the sitting room, which leads off to the left from the hall. . . ."

"How was she killed?"

"She was strangled. Yesterday morning, the lodgers were surprised not to hear her moving about downstairs as usual."

"She wasn't just here for the cure, then?"

"No, she lived in Vichy. . . . She owned the house, and let furnished rooms on the upper floor. . . ."

Maigret was still in his armchair, and his wife well knew just how much self-control was needed to keep him there.

"Was it a sex maniac?"

"The place was ransacked from top to bottom, but nothing seems to have been taken. . . . In one of the drawers that had been broken into, they found jewelry and quite a lot of money. . . ."

"She wasn't . . . ?"

"Raped? No."

He stared out of the window in silence.

"Who's in charge of the case, do you know?"

"Of course I don't! How could I?

"The Chief C.I.D. Officer at Clermont-Ferrand is Lecoeur, who used to work under me. . . . He's here. . . . Naturally, he has no idea that I'm here too. . . ."

"Will you be going to see him?"

To this he made no immediate answer.

2

It was five minutes to nine, and Maigret had not yet answered his wife's question. It seemed as though he had put himself on his honor to behave exactly as he would have done any other morning, to adhere, without the smallest deviation, to their established Vichy routine.

He had read the paper from beginning to end, while finishing his coffee. He had shaved and bathed, as usual, listening meanwhile to the news on the radio. At five minutes to nine he was ready, and together they went down the staircase, with its red carpet held in place by the triangular brass clips.

The proprietor, in white coat and chef's hat, was waiting for them below.

"Well, Monsieur Maigret, you can't say we don't look after you in Vichy, even to the extent of handing you a splendid murder on a platter. . . ."

He managed to force a noncommittal smile.

"You will be attending to it, I trust?"

"This is not Paris. I have no authority here. . . ."

Madame Maigret was watching him. She

33

thought he was unaware of this, but she was wrong. When they came to Rue d'Auvergne, he composed his features in an expression of guileless innocence and, instead of going down it toward the Allier and the children's playground, turned right.

Admittedly, they did occasionally take a different route, but, up to now, only on the way back. Her husband's unerring sense of direction never failed to astonish Madame Maigret. He never looked at a map, and would wander off, apparently at random, into a maze of little side streets. Often, just when it seemed to Madame Maigret that they must be lost, she would suddenly realize, with a start, that there in front of them was the door of their hotel, flanked on either side by the flowering shrubs in their green-painted urns.

On this occasion, he turned right again, and then again, until they came to a house where a small crowd was gathered, hoping to catch a glimpse inside.

There was a twinkle in Madame Maigret's eye. The Chief Superintendent, after a moment's hesitation, crossed the road, stopped, gave his pipe a sharp tap against his heel to knock out the ash, and then slowly filled it with fresh tobacco. At times like these, he seemed to her just a great baby, and a wave of tenderness swept over her.

He was having a struggle with himself. At last, trying to look as though he had no idea where he was, he joined the group of spectators, and stood gaping like the rest at the house across the street, where a policeman was standing guard and, nearby, a car was parked.

It was an attractive house, like most of the others in the street. It had recently had a fresh coat of warm-white paint, and the shutters and balcony were almond green.

On a marble plaque, in Gothic lettering, was inscribed the name: *Les Iris*.

Madame Maigret had been following every move in this little private drama, from his decision not to call at the Police Station to his present determination *not* to cross the road, make himself known to the policeman on duty, and gain admission to the house.

There was no cloud in the sky. The air was fresh, clear, invigorating, here in this clean little street. A few doors along, a woman, standing at her window shaking the dust out of her rugs, looked with disapproval at the people down below. But had she not herself been among the first, yesterday, when the murder was discovered and the police arrived in force, to join with her neighbors in gaping at a house that she had seen every day of her life for years?

Someone in the crowd remarked:

"They say it was a *crime passionel*."

This suggestion was received with derision:

"Oh, come! She can't have been a day under fifty."

A face could be dimly seen at one of the upstairs windows, a pointed nose, dark hair, and from time to time, behind it, the shadowy figure of a youngish man.

The door was painted white. A milk cart was moving slowly along the street, leaving bottles on doorsteps behind it. The milkman, with a bottle of milk in his hand, went up to the white door. The policman spoke to him, no doubt telling him that there was no point in leaving it, but the milkman shrugged and left the bottle just the same.

Wasn't anyone going to notice that Maigret . . .? He couldn't hang about here indefinitely. . . .

He was just about to move off when there appeared in the doorway a tall young man with an unruly mop of hair. He crossed the road, making straight for the Chief Superintendent.

"The Divisional Superintendent would very much like to see you, sir."

His wife, repressing a smile, asked:

"Where shall I wait for you?"

"At the usual place, the spring. . . ."

Had they seen and recognized him from the window? With dignity, he crossed the road, assuming a grumpy expression to hide his gratification. It was cool in the entrance. There was a hat-rack on the right, with two hats hanging from its branches. He added his own, a straw hat which his wife had made him buy at the same time as the mohair jacket, and in which he felt slightly foolish.

"Come on in, Chief."

A voice full of warm pleasure, a face and figure Maigret instantly recognized.

"Lecoeur!"

They had not met for fifteen years, not since the days when Désiré Lecoeur had been an inspector on Maigret's staff at the Quai des Orfèvres.

"Oh, yes, Chief, here I am, longer in the tooth, wider in girth, and higher up the ladder. Here I am, as I say, Divisional Superintendent at Clermont-Ferrand, which is why I'm stuck with this ghastly business. . . . Come on in."

He led him into a little parlor painted a bluish-gray, and sat at a table covered with papers, which he was using as an improvised desk.

Maigret lowered himself cautiously into a fragile, reproduction Louis XVI chair. Lecoeur must have noticed his puzzled expression, because he said at once:

"I daresay you're wondering how I knew you were here. In the first place, Moinet—you haven't met him, he's the head of the Vichy police—noticed the name on your registration form. . . . Naturally, he didn't want to intrude, but his men have seen you out and about every day. It seems, in fact, that the fellows doing duty on the beach have been laying bets as to when you would make up your mind to try your hand at bowls. Your interest in the game, according to them, was visibly growing, day by day. So much so that . . ."

"Have you been here since yesterday?"

"Yes, of course, with two of my men from Clermont-Ferrand. One of them is the young fellow, Dicelle, whom I sent out to fetch you when I saw you out there in the street. I was reluctant to send you a message at your hotel. I reckoned you were here for the cure, not for the purpose of giving us a helping hand. Besides, I knew that, in the end, if you were interested, you would . . ."

By now, Maigret really was looking grumpy.

"A sex maniac?" he mumbled.

"No, that's one thing we can say for sure."

"A jealous lover?"

"Unlikely. Mind you, I could be wrong. I've been at it for twenty-four hours, but I'm not much wiser than when I got here yesterday morning."

Referring from time to time to the papers on his desk, he went on:

"The murdered woman's was Hélène Lange. She was forty-eight years old, born at Marsilly, about ten miles from La Rochelle. I telephoned the town hall at Marsilly and was told that her mother, who was widowed very young, had for many years kept a small dry goods store in the Place de l'Eglise.

"There were two daughters. Hélène, the elder, took a course in shorthand and typing at La Rochelle. After that she worked for a time in a shipping office, and later went to Paris, after which nothing more was heard of her.

"No request for a copy of her birth certificate was ever received, from which one must infer that she never married, besides which her identity card is made out in her maiden name.

"There was a sister, six or seven years younger, who also began her working life in La Rochelle, as a manicurist.

"Like her elder sister, she subsequently migrated to Paris, but returned home about ten years ago.

"She must have had substantial savings, because she bought a hairdressing establishment in the Place des Armes, which she still owns. I tried to get her on the phone but was told by the assistant in charge that she was on holiday in Majorca. I cabled to her hotel, asking her to return immediately, and she should be here some time today.

"This sister—her name is Francine—is also unmarried. . . The mother has been dead eight years. . . . There's no other family, as far as anyone knows."

Quite unwittingly, Maigret had slipped back into his familiar professional role. To all appearances, he was in charge of the case, and Lecoeur was a subordinate reporting to him in his office.

But there was no pipe rack for him to fidget with as he listened, no sturdy armchair for him to lean back in, and no view of the Seine from the window.

As Lecoeur talked, Maigret was struck by one or two unusual features of this little parlor, which had obviously been used as a living room, in particular the fact that there were no photographs of anyone but Hélène Lange herself. There she was on a little bow-fronted chest, aged about six, in a dress that was too long for her, with tight braids hanging down on either side of her face.

A larger photograph, obviously taken by a skilled photographer, hung on the wall. In this she was older, about twenty, and her pose was romantic, her expression ethereal.

A third photograph showed her on a beach, wearing not a bathing suit but a white dress, the wide skirt of which, blown to one side by the breeze, streamed out like a flag, and holding in both hands a light, wide-brimmed hat.

"Do you know how and when the murder was committed?"

"We're having difficulty in finding out what exactly did happen that evening. . . . We've been working on it since yesterday morning, but we haven't made much headway.

"The night before last—Monday night, that is—

39

Hélène Lange had supper alone in her kitchen. She washed up—or at any rate we didn't find any dirty dishes in the sink—got dressed, switched off all the lights, and went out. If you want to know, she ate two boiled eggs. She wore a mauve dress, a white woolen shawl, and a hat, also white. . . ."

Maigret, after an internal struggle, couldn't in the end resist saying:

"I know.'"

"Have you been making inquiries, then?"

"No, but I saw her on Monday evening, sitting near the bandstand, listening to the concert."

"Do you know what time she left?"

"She was still there just before half past nine, when my wife and I went for our walk, as we do every evening."

"Was she alone?"

"She was always alone."

Lecoeur made no attempt to hide his astonishment.

"So you'd noticed her on other occasions?"

Maigret, now looking much more good-humored, nodded.

"What was it about her?"

"Nothing in particular. One spends one's time here just walking about, and, almost unconsciously, one registers a face here and there in the crowd. You know how it is . . . one is always running into the same people in the same places at certain times of day. . . ."

"Have you any ideas?"

"What about?"

"What sort of woman she was."

"She was no ordinary woman, I'm sure of that, but that's all I can say."

"Well, to proceed ... Two of the three bedrooms on the upper floor are let, the largest to the Maleskis, a couple from Grenoble. He's an engineer. They were out at the cinema. They left the house a few minutes after Mademoiselle Lange and didn't get back till half past eleven. All the shutters were closed as usual, but they could see through the slats that the lights were still on downstairs. When they got inside, they noticed strips of light under the doors of Mademoiselle Lange's living room and bedroom. That's the room on the right. . . ."

"Did they hear anything?"

"Maleski heard nothing, but his wife said, with some hesitation, that she thought she had heard a murmur of voices. . . . They went straight up to bed, and slept undisturbed until morning. . . .

"The other lodger is a Madame Vireveau, a widow from Paris, Rue Lamarck. She's rather an overbearing woman, aged about sixty. She comes to Vichy every year to lose weight. . . . This is the first time she's taken a room in Mademoiselle Lange's house. In former years she always stayed at a hotel.

"She's seen better days, apparently. Her husband was a rich man, but extravagant, and when he died she found herself in financial difficulties. . . . To put it briefly, she's loaded with imitation jewelry, and she booms like a dowager in a bad play. . . . She left the house at nine. She saw no one, and claims that, when she went out, the house was in total darkness."

"Do the lodgers have their own keys?"

"Yes. Madame Vireveau spent the evening at the Carlton Bridge Club, and left just before midnight. She hasn't a car. The Maleskis have a mini, but they seldom use it in Vichy. Most of the time it's left in a garage nearby. . . ."

"Were the lights still on?"

"I'm coming to that, Chief. Naturally, I saw the old girl only after the crime had been discovered, and by then the whole street was in a turmoil. . . . Maybe all that fancy jewelry goes with a vivid imagination . . . I really can't say. . . . Anyway, according to her story, she almost bumped into a man as she turned the corner, the corner of Boulevard de LaSalle and Rue du Bourbonnais, that is. He couldn't possibly have seen her coming, and she swears that he was visibly startled, and shielded his face with his hand to avoid being recognized."

"Did she, in fact, recognize him?"

"No, but she swears nevertheless that she would recognize him if she saw him again face to face. He was very tall and heavily built—with a great bulging chest like a gorilla, she says. He was hunched up and walking fast. He gave her a real fright, she says, but all the same she turned back to watch him striding away toward the center of town."

"Had she any idea of his age?"

"Not young . . . Not old, either . . . Very heavily built . . . Frightening. . . . She almost ran the rest of the way. She didn't feel safe until her key was in the lock. . . ."

42

"Were the lights still showing on the ground floor?"

"That's just it, they weren't, that is, if one can take her word for it. She didn't hear a thing. She went up to bed, so shaken that she had to take a teaspoonful of peppermint essence on a lump of sugar."

"Who discovered the body?"

"All in good time, Chief. Mademoiselle Lange, while quite willing to let her rooms to respectable people, was not prepared to serve meals. No cooking was allowed. She wouldn't even let them have an alcohol stove for a cup of morning coffee.

"Yesterday morning, at about eight, Madame Maleski came downstairs with her thermos flask, as she always did, to get it filled and buy some croissants at a nearby coffee bar. She didn't notice anything amiss, then or when she got back. What did surprise her, though, was the absolute quiet downstairs, especially the second time, because Mademoiselle Lange was an early riser and could usually be heard moving about from one room to another.

" 'Perhaps she's not well,' she remarked to her husband over breakfast.

"Because it seems that the landlady often complained of poor health. At nine o'clock—Madame Vireveau was still in her room—the Maleskis went downstairs, where they found Charlotte looking worried. . . ."

"Charlotte?"

"The girl who comes in every morning from nine to twelve to clean the rooms. She bicycles in

43

from a village about ten miles away. She's a bit simple.

" 'All the doors are locked,' she said to the Maleskis.

"Usually she arrived to find all the doors and windows on the ground floor wide open; Mademoiselle Lange was a great one for fresh air."

" 'Haven't you got a key?'

" 'No, if she's not in, I might as well go home.'

"Maleski tried to open the door with the key of his room, but it didn't fit, so in the end he went to the coffee bar where his wife gets their breakfast, and called the police from there.

"And that's about all. An inspector from Vichy Police Headquarters arrived within minutes with a locksmith. The key to the living-room door was missing, and the kitchen and bedroom doors were locked from inside, with the keys in the locks.

"They found Hélène Lange here, in this room. She was lying stretched out, or rather doubled up, on the edge of the carpet, here in this exact spot. She had been strangled. . . . It wasn't a pretty sight. . . .

"She was still wearing her mauve dress, but she had taken off her hat and shawl, which were both found hanging on the hatrack in the hall. All the drawers were open, and there were papers and cardboard boxes scattered all over the floor."

"Had she been raped?"

"No, nothing of that sort was even attempted. And as far as we know, nothing was stolen. The report in this morning's *Journal* is reasonably accurate. . . . In one of the drawers we found five hundred-franc notes. . . . The assailant had been

44

through the dead woman's handbag, and the contents were scattered about the room. These included four hundred francs in small notes, some silver, and a season ticket for the Grand Casino theater...."

"Has she lived here long?"

"Nine years. Before that she lived for some years in Nice...."

"Did she work there?"

"No. She lived in rather a shabby lodginghouse in Boulevard Albert I. Presumably she had a small private income."

"Did she travel at all?"

"She was in the habit of going away about once a month, for a day or two at a time."

"Do you know where she went?"

"She was very secretive about her comings and goings."

"And after she came here?"

"For the first two years she had the whole house to herself. Then she advertised three rooms to let during the season, but the house was not always full. Just now, for instance, the blue room isn't let.... I should perhaps mention that each bedroom has a different color scheme. Besides the blue room, there are a white room and a pink room."

At this point, Maigret suddenly noticed another odd thing. Nowhere in the living room was there the smallest touch of green, not a single ornament or cushion, not even a trimming.

"Was she superstitious?"

"How did you guess? One day she got into quite a state because Madame Maleski had brought home a bunch of carnations. She said they were flowers of ill-omen, and she wouldn't have them in the house.

"On another occasion she warned Madame Vireveau against wearing a green dress, prophesying that she would pay dearly for it. . . ."

"Did she ever have visitors?"

"According to the neighbors, never."

"Any mail?"

"We've spoken to the postman. There was an occasional letter from La Rochelle, but apart from that, nothing but circulars and bills from local shops."

"Did she have a bank account?"

"With the Crédit Lyonnais, on the corner of Rue Georges-Clemenceau."

"You've made inquiries there, of course?"

"She deposited regularly, about five thousand francs a month, but not always on the same day of the month."

"In cash?"

"Yes. During the season she deposited more, because of the money coming in from the lodgers."

"Did she ever sign checks?"

"There were a number of checks made out to shops in Vichy and Moulins, where she sometimes went to do her shopping. Occasionally she would order something from Paris—something she had seen in a mail-order catalogue: look, there's a pile of them over there—and for these things, too, she would pay by check."

Lecoeur was watching the Chief Superintendent and thinking how different he looked, in his off-white jacket, from the man he had worked for in the Quai des Orfèvres.

"What do you make of it, Chief?"

"I'll have to be going. My wife is waiting for me."

"Not to mention your first glass of water!"

"So the Vichy police know about that too, do they?" grumbled Maigret.

"But you'll be back, won't you? The C.I.D. hasn't a branch in Vichy. I drive back to Clermont-Ferrand every night. It's only fifty miles. The Vichy Chief of Police has offered me the use of an office with a telephone, but I'd sooner have my headquarters here on the spot. My men are trying to trace any neighbors or passers-by who may have seen Mademoiselle Lange returning home on Monday night, because we still don't know whether the murderer came with her or was waiting for her in the house."

"Forgive me, my dear fellow.... My wife ..."

"Of course, Chief."

Maigret was still determined to stick to his routine, though curiosity very nearly got the better of him. He felt he really ought not to have turned right instead of left when setting out from the Hôtel de la Bérézina. Had he not done so, he would have lingered, as always up till now, in the children's playground, and then, farther on, stopped to watch a game or two of bowls.

He wondered whether Madame Maigret, all on her own, had followed the familiar route, stopping at all the places where they usually stopped together.

"Would you care for a lift? My car is at the

47

door, and I'm sure there's nothing young Dicelle would like better than to . . ."

"No, thank you, I shall walk. That's what I'm here for."

And walk he did, alone, striding along at a brisk pace to make up for lost time.

He had drunk his first glass of water and returned to his seat, midway between the great glass hall built around the spring and the nearest tree. Although his wife asked no questions, he could feel her watching his every movement, trying to interpret his expression.

With the newspapers spread out on his lap, he sat gazing at the sky through the trees. There was scarcely any movement among the leaves, and the sky was still the same clear blue, with one small solitary cloud, dazzlingly white, drifting across it.

Sometimes in Paris he would feel a twinge of nostalgia for half-forgotten sensory experiences: a puff of wind, warmed by the sun, against his cheek, the play of light among leaves or on a gravel path, the crunch of gravel under running feet, even the taste of dust.

And here, miraculously, they all were. While reflecting on his meeting with Lecoeur, he was at the same time basking in his surroundings, savoring every little thing.

Was he really deep in thought, or just daydreaming? There were small family groups to be seen here and there, as there are everywhere, but in this place the proportion of elderly couples was greater.

And what about the solitary figures in the

crowd? Were there more men than women? Women, especially old women, tend to be gregarious. They could be seen arranging their chairs in little groups of six or eight, leaning forward as though to exchange confidences, although they had probably known one another not more than a few days.

Were they really exchanging confidences? Who could say? No doubt they discussed their illnesses, their doctors, their treatment, and went on to talk about their married sons and daughters, and to display the photographs of their grandchildren, which they carried about in their handbags.

It was uncommon to see one of them remaining aloof, keeping herself to herself, like the lady in lilac, to whom he could now attach a name.

Solitary men were more numerous. Often these showed signs of exhaustion and pain, and it was an obvious effort for them to move with dignity among the crowd. Their drawn features and sad eyes bespoke a vague, distressed apprehension that they might crumple to the ground, and lie there in a patch of sunlight or shade, in among the legs of the people passing by.

Hélène Lange was one of the solitary ones, and everything about her, her expression, her bearing, told that she was a proud woman. She would not allow herself to be treated as an old maid, she would not accept pity. She went her way, very erect, chin held high, walking with a firm tread.

She consorted with no one, having no need of the relief of facile confidences.

Was it by choice that she had lived alone?

This was the question uppermost in his mind, as he tried to conjure up an image of her as he had seen her, sitting, standing, in motion, still.

"Have they any clue?"

Madame Maigret was beginning to feel a little aggrieved at his daydreaming. In Paris she would never have dared question her husband while he was working on a case. But here it was different. Here, walking side by side for hours on end, they had got into the habit of thinking aloud.

They did not converse exactly, exchanging question and answer, but rather one or the other would occasionally let fall the odd, disjointed phrase to indicate what he or she was thinking.

"No. They can't do much until the sister gets here."

"Has she no other family?"

"Apparently not."

"It's time for your second glass."

They went into the hall. The heads of the girl attendants showed above the sides of the well in which they stood. Hélène Lange came here every day to take the waters. Was this on medical advice, or was it just to give some point to her morning walk?

"What's bothering you?"

"I'm wondering why Vichy."

It was almost ten years since she had come to settle in the town, and had bought her house. She was therefore thirty-seven at the time, and must have had independent means, since it was not until she had had the house to herself for two years that she started letting rooms.

"Why not Vichy?" retorted Madame Maigret.

"There are hundreds of towns in France, small towns, larger towns, where she might have gone to settle, not to mention La Rochelle, where she grew up. . . . Her sister, having spent some time in Paris, went back to La Rochelle and stayed there. . . ."

"Perhaps the two sisters didn't get on."

It wasn't as simple as that. Maigret was still watching the people strolling about. The tempo of the moving crowds reminded him of something, of a constant stream of people, ebbing and flowing in hot sunshine. In Nice, on the Promenade des Anglais.

For Hélène Lange, before coming to Vichy, had lived five years in Nice.

"She lived five years in Nice," he said, speaking his thoughts aloud.

"Like a lot of other people on small fixed incomes."

"Exactly. . . . People on small fixed incomes, but also people from all walks of life, the same as here. . . . Only the day before yesterday I was trying to remember what I was reminded of by the crowds strolling in the park and sitting on the chairs. . . . They're just like the crowds on the seafront at Nice . . . an agglomeration of elements so diverse that they cancel each other out. Vichy, like Nice, must surely have its share of superannuated sirens, former stars of stage and screen. . . . You've seen for yourself the streets of opulent private villas, where there are actually footmen in striped waistcoats still.

"And up in the hills, well away from the public gaze, there are villas even more opulent."

"As in Nice. . . . And what do you deduce from that?"

"Nothing. She was thirty-two when she went to live in Nice, and she was as much on her own there as she was here. Solitude doesn't, as a rule, come so early in life."

"There are such things as unhappy love affairs."

"Yes, but the sufferers don't look as she did."

"Broken marriages are not unknown."

"Ninety-five per cent of those women remarry."

"What about the men?"

With a broad grin, he retorted:

"A hundred per cent!"

She could not be sure whether he was teasing her or not.

Nice has a floating population, several casinos, and branches of nearly all the main Paris shops. Vichy virtually changes its population every three weeks, as the hundreds of thousands taking the cure come and go. It has branches of the same shops, three casinos, and a dozen cinemas.

Anywhere else, she would have been known. People would have taken an interest in her, they would have pried into her mode of life, her comings and goings.

Not in Nice. Not in Vichy. Was it that she had something to hide?

"Are you going back to see Lecoeur?"

"He said to come whenever I felt like it. He calls me 'Chief,' just as though he were still working under me."

"They all do."

"That's true. It's just habit, I daresay."

"You don't think it could be affection?"

He shrugged, and suggested that it was time they were on their way. This time, they went through the old town, stopping to look in the windows of the antique shops, where so many old and some touchingly pathetic objects were displayed.

In the dining room they were conscious of being stared at by their fellow guests. Oh, well, they would just have to get used to it.

Maigret had conscientiously modified his eating habits in accordance with the doctor's instructions: chew everything thoroughly before swallowing, even mashed potatoes; never replenish your fork until you have swallowed the previous mouthful; do not drink more than a couple of sips of water with your meals, flavored with a drop of wine, if you must.

He preferred to do without wine altogether.

On the way upstairs he permitted himself a couple of puffs at his pipe, before stretching out, fully dressed, for his afternoon rest. His wife sat in the armchair by the window. There was just enough light coming in through the slats in the blinds to enable her to read the paper, as he had done earlier. From time to time, as he lay dozing, he could hear the rustle of a page being turned.

He had been resting for barely twenty minutes when there was a knock at the door. Madame Maigret got up hastily and went out, shutting the door behind her. After a whispered consultation, she went downstairs. She was back within minutes.

"It was Lecoeur."

"Any fresh news?"

"The sister has just arrived in Vichy. She went straight to the Police Station. She's about to be taken to the mortuary, to make a formal identification. Lecoeur will be waiting to see her in Rue du Bourbonnais. He thought you might like to be present when he questioned her."

Maigret, grumbling to himself, was already on his feet. For a start, he would have the shutters open, to let a little light and life into the place.

"Shall we meet at the spring?"

Five o'clock in the afternoon: the spring, the first glass of water, the iron chair.

"It won't take that long. You'd better wait for me on one of the benches near the bowling greens."

He was looking dubiously at his straw hat.

"What's the matter? Are you afraid of being laughed at?"

Well, let them laugh. He was on holiday, wasn't he? Defiantly, he put it on.

The same policeman was on guard outside the house. There were still a good many people about, drawn there by curiosity, but when they found that there was nothing to be seen through the closed windows, most of them moved off, shaking their heads.

"Take a seat, Chief. If you move your chair into that corner over there by the window, you'll be able to see her with the light full on her."

"Have you seen her yet?"

"I was in a restaurant having lunch—and a very good lunch it was, I must say—when I got a message that she was at the Police Station. They said they'd see to it that she was taken to the mortuary, and brought on here afterward."

And at that moment they saw, through the net curtains, a black car with a policeman in uniform at the wheel and, following behind, a long, red, open sports car. It was plain from their disheveled hair and tanned faces that the man and woman in the front seats had just got back from holiday.

The couple talked for a minute or two, their heads close together. They exchanged a hurried kiss, and she got out of the car and slammed the door. Her companion, still sitting at the wheel, lit a cigarette.

He was dark, with strong features and athletic shoulders, which were clearly outlined under his close-fitting, yellow, polo-neck sweater. He was surveying the house with a bored expression, when the policeman ushered the young woman into the living room.

"I am Superintendent Lecoeur.... You are Francine Lange, I presume?"

"That's right."

She glanced briefly at Maigret, whose face was in shadow, and to whom she had not been introduced.

"Madame or Mademoiselle?"

"I'm not married, if that's what you mean. I have a friend with me; he's in the car. But I know too much about men to marry one of them. It's the devil's own job to get rid of them afterward...."

She was a fine-looking woman, who appeared much younger than her forty years, and her provocative curves seemed out of place in this conventional little room. She was wearing a flame-colored dress of material so thin that her bare flesh showed through it, and the salt tang of the sea seemed still to cling to her.

"I got your telegram last night. Lucien managed to get seats on the first plane to Paris. . . . We had left our car at Orly, so we drove the rest of the way from there. . . ."

"I take it she was, indeed, your sister?"

Showing no sign of emotion, she nodded.

"Won't you sit down?"

"Thank you. Do you mind if I smoke?"

She looked meaningfully at the smoke rising up from Maigret's pipe, as if to say:

"If he can smoke, what's to stop me?"

"Please do. . . . I take it you were no more prepared for this murder than we were?"

"Well, naturally, I wasn't expecting it!"

"Do you know of anyone who might have had a grudge against your sister?"

"Why should anyone have had a grudge against Hélène?"

"When did you see her last?"

"Six or seven years ago, I can't say exactly. . . . It was winter, I remember, and there was a storm raging. . . . She hadn't let me know she was coming, so I was taken by surprise when she coolly walked into my hairdressing salon."

"Did you get on well together?"

"As well as most sisters. . . . We never saw much of one another, because of the difference in our ages. . . . When I was starting school, she had just left. . . . Then she went to the Secretarial School in La Rochelle. . . . I didn't train as a manicurist till years after. . . . Later, she left the town."

56

"How old was she then?"

"Let me think.... I was in the second year of my training ... so I must have been sixteen.... She was seven years older.... That would make her twenty-three...."

"Did you correspond?"

"Very rarely.... We don't go in much for letter-writing in our family."

"Was your mother still alive then?"

"Yes ... she died two years later, and Hélène came to Marsilly for the division of her property.... Not that there was much to divide.... The shop was almost worthless...."

"What was your sister doing in Paris?"

Maigret never took his eyes off her, making a mental comparison, line by line, between her face and figure and those of the dead woman. There was very little resemblance between the two women, the dark-eyed, long-jawed Hélène and the blue-eyed Francine, who was almost certainly not a natural blonde, with that bizarre streak of fiery red dangling over her forehead.

At first sight she seemed a good sort, hail-fellow-well-met with her clientele, no doubt, exuberantly cheerful if a little coarse. She made no pretense of refinement, indeed she seemed bent on accentuating her natural vulgarity, almost as if she relished it.

It was not half an hour since she had viewed her sister's body in the mortuary, yet here she was answering Lecoeur's questions good-humoredly, almost gaily, and—probably just from habit—attempting to make a conquest of him.

"What was she doing in Paris? Working as a

stenographer in an office presumably, though I never went there to find out.... We had very little in common. I was just fifteen when I had my first boy friend—a taxi driver, he was—and I've had a good many since.... I don't think that was Hélène's style at all, unless she was a very dark horse...."

"What address did you write to?"

"At the beginning, as far as I remember, it was a hotel in Avenue de Clichy.... I forget the name.... She moved several times.... Later she took an apartment in Rue Notre-Dame-de-Lorette.... I can't remember the number."

"You yourself went to live in Paris after a time.... Did you never go and see her?"

"Yes, I did. She was living in Rue Notre-Dame-de-Lorette by then. A very nice little apartment it was. I was amazed.... I remember remarking on it.... She had a large bedroom looking out on the street, a living room, a kitchenette, and a real bathroom...."

"Was there a man in her life?"

"I never found out. I wanted to stay a few days with her, while I looked for a suitable room. She said she knew of a very clean, modestly priced hotel where I could stay, but she couldn't bear to have anyone living with her."

"Not even for three or four days?"

"Apparently not."

"Did it surprise you?"

"Not all that much.... I may say, it takes a lot to surprise me.... I don't like other people to meddle in my affairs, and I don't interfere in theirs."

"How long were you in Paris?"

"Eleven years."

"Working as a manicurist?"

"To begin with. I worked in several salons in the neighborhood, and then I moved to a beauty parlor in Champs-Elysées. That was where I trained as a beauty specialist."

"Were you living alone?"

"Sometimes alone, sometimes not."

"Did you see anything of your sister?"

"To all intents and purposes, nothing."

"So that you can't really tell us anything about her life in Paris?"

"All I know is that she had a job. . . ."

"When you returned to La Rochelle to open your own salon, did you have much in the way of savings?"

"A fair amount."

He did not ask how she had earned this money, nor did she volunteer the information, but she probably took it for granted that he understood.

"You never married?"

"I've answered that already. I'm not such a fool as to . . ."

And, turning to the window, from which they could see her companion lounging at the wheel of the red sports car:

"He looks like a real lout, don't you think?"

"And yet you're living with him. . . ."

"He works for me, and what's more, he's a first-class hairdresser. We don't live together in La Rochelle; I wouldn't want him around all night as well as all day. . . . On holiday, it's different. . . ."

"Is the car yours?"

"Of course."

"But he chose it?"

"How did you guess?"

"Did your sister ever have a child?"

"Why do you ask?"

"I don't know . . . she was a woman. . . ."

"Not to my knowledge, she didn't. . . . I shouldn't have thought it was the kind of thing you could hide. . . ."

"What about you?"

"I had a child while I was living in Paris. Fifteen years ago . . . My first thought was to get rid of it. . . . It would have been better if I had. . . . It was my sister who urged me not to. . . ."

"So you were in touch with her then?"

"It was because of it that I went to see her. . . . I needed someone to talk to—a member of my own family. . . . You may think it silly, but there are times when one instinctively turns to one's family. . . . Anyway, I had a son, Philippe. . . . I put him out to foster parents in the Vosges. . . ."

"Why the Vosges? Did you have any ties there?"

"None whatever. Hélène saw an advertisement somewhere or other. . . . I used to go and see him. . . . I suppose I went about ten times in two years. . . . He was well cared for. . . . The foster parents were very kind. . . . They had a small farm, beautifully kept. . . . Then one day I heard from them that the child was dead, drowned in a pond. . . ."

She was silent and thoughtful for a moment or two, then she shrugged:

"All things considered, it was probably for the best. . . ."

"Did you know of no one who was close to your sister, man or woman?"

"I doubt if she had many friends. Even in the old days in Marsilly she looked down her nose at the other girls. They used to call her the Princess. . . . It was no different, I imagine, at the Secretarial School in La Rochelle. . . ."

"Was it pride?"

She thought this over, then said uncertainly:

"I don't know. . . . That's not the word I would choose. . . . She didn't like people. . . . She didn't like the company of other people. . . . That's it! She was happiest on her own."

"Did she ever attempt suicide?"

"Why should she? You don't think . . ."

Lecoeur smiled.

"No, no one commits suicide by strangulation. . . . I just wondered whether, at any time in the past, she had been tempted to put an end to her life."

"I'm sure it never entered her head. . . . She had a good opinion of herself. Basically, she was very self-satisfied."

Yes, thought Maigret, that was it, self-satisfied. In his mind's eye he saw once again the lady in lilac sitting facing the bandstand. At the time, he had tried to interpret her expression, and failed.

Francine had put her finger on it: self-satisfaction.

She was so self-absorbed that she kept no less than three photographs of herself in her living room, and no doubt there were others in the dining room and bedroom, which he had not yet seen. She had no photograph of anyone else. None of her mother, none of her sister, none of any friend, man or woman. Even on the beach she had been photographed alone, against a background of waves.

"I take it that, as far as you know, you are her sole heir? . . . We found no will among her papers. Admittedly, the murderer scattered them all over the place, but I can't imagine any reason why he should have made off with her will. . . . So far, we have heard nothing from any lawyer. . . ."

"When is the funeral to be?"

"That's up to you. The forensic laboratory have completed their work, so you can claim your sister's body whenever you wish."

"Where do you think she should be buried?"

"I haven't the least idea."

"I don't know a soul here. . . . If I took her back to Marsilly the whole village would turn out for the funeral—to gape. . . . I wonder if it really would have been her wish to end up in Marsilly. . . . Look, if you don't need me any more, I'd like to go and book into a hotel. I'm longing for a good hot bath. . . . Let me think it over, and tomorrow morning . . ."

"Very well. I shall expect to see you tomorrow morning."

Just as she was leaving, having shaken hands with Lecoeur, she turned to glance briefly at Maigret. She was frowning, as though puzzled by the presence of this silent man sitting in shadow.

Did she recognize him?

"Till tomorrow, then. You have been most kind."

They saw her get into the car and lean over to say something to her companion at the wheel, and then the car drove off.

In the living room the two men looked at one another. Lecoeur was the first to speak:

"Well?" he said. It was almost comical.

And Maigret, puffing at his pipe, retorted:

"Well, what?"

He didn't feel like discussing the case. Besides, he hadn't forgotten that he had promised to meet his wife near the bowling greens.

"I must be going, my dear fellow. I'll see you tomorrow."

"Till tomorrow, then."

The policeman's military salute was no more than was due to him. All the same, he felt a glow of pride.

3

He was back in his old place, sitting in the green armchair near the open window. The weather had not changed since the day they arrived, warm sunshine in abundance, yet with a cool breeze at the start of the day, when the municipal sprinkler-carts made their rounds of the streets. And later on it would be pleasantly cool in the shade of the thickly wooded park, the many tree-lined boulevards, and the Allier promenade.

He had eaten his three croissants. His coffee cup was still half full. His wife was having her bath next door, and on the floor below he could hear the sounds of people moving about their rooms, getting ready to go downstairs.

It was not without a touch of wry amusement that he noted how quickly he had formed new habits. That was always his way. Wherever he was, he would almost instinctively establish a routine, and then adhere to it, as though subject to some immutable law.

It would be true to say that, when he was in Paris, each separate investigation had a tempo of its own, which included periods of rest in one particular bistro or brasserie, with its own characteristic smells and quality of light.

Here, in Vichy, he felt much more like a man on holiday than a man taking the cure, and even the death of the lady in lilac had failed to shatter his indolent mood.

The night before, they had gone for their customary walk in the park, where several hundred others like themselves appeared as dark shadows, except when they moved through a pool of light cast by one of the frosted globes of the lamp standards. At this hour, most people were at the theater, the cinema, or the casino. Everywhere, after a light meal of cold ham, people were coming out of their hotels, pensions, and lodgings, in search of their own chosen form of entertainment.

Many were quite happy just to sit and relax on the florid little yellow chairs, and Maigret, without thinking, had caught himself searching in the crowd for an erect and dignified figure, a face with a long jaw line, a chin held high, and an expression that was at once wistful and hard.

Hélène Lange was dead, and Francine, no doubt, was consulting with her gigolo as to where she should have her sister buried.

Somewhere in this town there was a man who could solve the mystery of the lonely woman who owned a house called *Les Iris*, the man who had strangled her.

Was he taking his customary walk in the park, or was he, at this minute, on his way to the theater or the cinema?

Maigret and his wife had undressed and gone

65

to bed in silence, but each had known what the other was thinking.

He lit his pipe and opened his paper at the section devoted to local news.

A photograph of himself spread over two columns caused him to draw in his breath sharply. It was a recent photograph, showing him drinking one of his daily glasses of water. He could not imagine when it had been taken. His wife had been sitting beside him at this time—they had left in about a third of her—and in the background were several blurred, anonymous faces.

MAIGRET TO THE RESCUE?

Out of consideration for his privacy, we have not hitherto informed our readers of the presence among us of Chief Superintendent Maigret. He is in Vichy in a private capacity, having come, like so many other distinguished public figures, to take advantage of the beneficial properties of our mineral springs.

The question now arises, will the Chief Superintendent be able to resist the temptation to try his hand at solving the mystery of Rue du Bourbonnais?

He has been seen in the neighborhood of the house where the murder was committed, and rumor has it that he is in touch with Superintendent Lecoeur, the popular head of C.I.D., Clermont-Ferrand, who is in charge of the case.

With loyalties divided between the cure and the case, which will he choose?

He dropped the paper with a shrug. He was used to personal gossip of this sort, and it no longer angered him. He turned, and stared absent-mindedly out of the window.

Up to now—it was nine o'clock—he had behaved exactly as he did every morning, and when Madame Maigret reappeared, wearing her pink suit, they went downstairs as usual.

"Monsieur, madame, good morning...." As usual, the proprietor was there to greet them. Maigret had already seen the two men outside, and the glint of their camera lens.

"They've been waiting for you for the past hour. They're from the Saint-Etienne *Tribune*, not from the local paper."

The photographer was tall, with red hair. The man with him, small and dark, had one shoulder higher than the other. They ran up to the door.

"May we take a picture? Just one?"

What was the use of saying no? He stood quite still for a moment on the doorstep, between the two flowering shrubs, Madame Maigret having retreated into the shadows.

"Look up, please, sir. Your hat ..."

He could not remember when he had last been photographed wearing a straw hat. The only other he now possessed was the one he kept at Meung-sur-Loire for gardening.

"One more.... It won't take a second. Thank you...."

"Just one question, Monsieur Maigret, is it true that you are taking part in the investigation?"

"As Chief of the Criminal Investigation Department at the Quai des Orfèvres, I have no authority here."

"All the same, you must be taking an interest?"

"No more than all your other readers."

"It has one or two peculiar features, don't you think?"

"What do you mean?"

"The victim was a recluse.... She had no friends.... There is no obvious motive...."

"When we know more about her, the motive, no doubt, will become apparent."

It was not a particularly profound remark, and it committed him to nothing, but, all the same, it contained a germ of essential truth. For a long time now, others besides Maigret have seen the importance of studying the character of the victim. Increasingly, the attention of criminologists has centered upon the dead person, even to the extent of laying a large share of the blame at the victim's door.

Might there not have been something in Hélène Lange's manner and way of life which had, in a sense, doomed her to death by violence? From the very first, when he had seen her under the trees in the park, the Chief Superintendent had fixed upon her as an object of interest.

True, she was not the only one. The two whom he and his wife always referred to as "the happy pair" had also aroused his interest.

"Isn't it a fact that Superintendent Lecoeur used to be on your staff?"

"He did work for a time in the Law Courts in Paris."

"Have you seen him?"

"I paid him a friendly call."

"Will you be seeing him again?"

"Very likely."

"Will you be discussing the murder with him?"

"Very likely. Unless we confine ourselves to the weather, and the strange quality of the light in your charming town."

"What's so strange about it?"

"It's soft and shimmering at one and the same time."

"Do you intend to come back to Vichy next year?"

"That depends on my doctor."

"Many thanks. . . ."

As the two men leapt into their battered motorcar, Maigret and his wife walked slowly away from the hotel.

"Where shall I wait for you?"

She took it for granted that her husband was going to Rue du Bourbonnais.

"At the spring?"

"At the bowling greens."

In other words, he didn't intend to stay long with Lecoeur. He found him in the tiny parlor, talking on the telephone.

"Take a seat, Chief. . . . Hello! . . . Yes. . . . It's a bit of luck finding the same concierge there after all these years. . . . Yes. . . . She doesn't know where? . . . She went by métro? . . . From Saint-Georges? . . . Don't cut us off, miss. . . . Carry on, chum. . . ."

The call lasted for another two or three minutes.

"Thanks. . . . I'll see you get a formal authorization, just for the record. You can send us your report then. . . . How's the wife? . . . Of course. There's always something to worry about with kids. . . . I should know, with four boys of my own. . . ."

He hung up and turned to Maigret.

"That was Julien. He's an inspector in the IXth

Arrondissement now.... You must have known him.... I called him up yesterday, and he agreed to look through his departmental files.... He's located the place in Rue Notre-Dame-de-Lorette where Hélène Lange lived for four years."

"From the age of twenty-eight to thirty-two, in fact...."

"Roughly.... The concierge is still there.... Mademoiselle Lange, it seems, was a nice, quiet young woman.... She went out and came back at regular hours, as one would expect of a working girl.... It seems that she seldom went out in the evenings, except occasionally to the theater or cinema.

"Her place of work must have been some distance away, as she used the métro.... She always went out early to do her shopping, and she had no domestic help.... She usually got home for lunch at about twenty past twelve, and left again at half past one. After that she wasn't seen again until she got back from work at half past six."

"Did she have any visitors?"

"Only one, a man. Always the same man."

"Did you get his name from the concierge?"

"She knew nothing about him, except that he used to call once or twice a week at about half past eight at night, and always left before ten."

"What sort of man?"

"Very respectable, according to her. He drove his own car. It never occurred to the concierge to make a note of the number. It was a large black car, American, I imagine."

"What age?"

"In his forties. . . . On the heavy side. . . . Very well groomed. . . . Expensive clothes. . . ."

"Was he paying the rent?"

"He never set foot in the concierge's lodge."

"Did they go away together for weekends?"

"Only once."

"What about holidays?"

"No. . . . At that time, Hélène Lange only got two weeks' holiday, and she nearly always went to Etretat, staying in a family pension, to which her mail was forwarded."

"Did she get many letters?"

"Very few. . . . One from her sister occasionally. . . . She subscribed to a lending library nearby. She was a great reader."

"Do you mind if I take a look around the apartment?"

"Of course not. Make yourself at home, Chief."

He noted that the television set was not in the little parlor, but in the dining room, which was furnished in provincial style, with the inevitable brass hardware much in evidence. On the sideboard was a photograph of Hélène Lange bowling a hoop, and another of her in a bathing suit, with a cliff in the background, probably taken at Etretat. She had a well-proportioned figure, the long slender lines of the face being carried through to the body, though she was by no means thin or sharp. She was one of those women to whom clothes are unflattering.

In the kitchen, which was modern and bright, there was a dishwasher, not to mention every other labor-saving appliance.

Across the hall was a bathroom, also modern

and well equipped, and the dead woman's bed-room.

Maigret was amused to find that it was almost a replica of his own bedroom, with the same style of brass bedstead and the same elaborately carved furniture. The wallpaper was striped, lavender blue and pale pink, and here too hung a photo-graph of Hélène Lange, taken when she was about thirty.

But he scarcely recognized, behind that wide, spontaneous, joyous smile, the secretive face he had come to know.

It was an enlarged snapshot, probably taken in a wood, if the foliage in the background was any-thing to go by. She was looking straight into the lens, her features softened in an expression almost of tenderness.

"It would be interesting to know who it was holding the camera," mumbled Maigret to Le-coeur, who had just come into the room.

"A bit of a mystery, isn't she?"

"I take it you've checked up on the lodgers?"

"It was my first idea, too, that it might be an inside job. The widow is in the clear, and any-way, in spite of her bulk, she wouldn't have the strength to strangle anyone who put up a fight like Mademoiselle Lange. . . . The Carlton staff confirm that she was there playing bridge until twenty past eleven. . . . And, according to the po-lice surgeon, the murder was committed between ten and eleven. . . ."

"In other words, by the time Madame Vireveau got home, Hélène Lange was dead."

"Almost certainly.

"The Maleskis saw a light under the living-room door. . . . It follows, since the lights were later turned off, that the murderer was still in the apartment. . . .

"That's what I keep telling myself. . . . Either he came in with his victim and strangled her before searching the apartment, or she found him at it, and had to be silenced. . . ."

"What about the man Madame Vireveau claims to have seen on the corner?"

"We're working on that. Just about that time, as the proprietor of a nearby bar was pulling down his iron shutter, he saw a heavily built man walking rapidly past. He seemed out of breath, he says. . . ."

"Which way was he going?"

"Toward the Célestins."

"Did he describe him?"

"He wasn't paying much attention. . . . All he could say was that he was wearing a dark suit and no hat. . . . He thinks he remembers noticing that he had receding hair."

"Any anonymous letters?"

"Not so far."

There would be. There had never been a crime with a bit of mystery to it that did not produce its crop of anonymous letters and cryptic telephone calls.

"Have you seen the sister again?"

"I'm still waiting to hear from her what she wants done with the body."

And, after a brief pause, he added:

"You could scarcely find two sisters more un-like, could you? The one so reserved, so introverted, so superior, and the other a thoroughgoing extrovert, overflowing with health and vitality. . . . And yet . . ."

Maigret looked at Lecoeur with an indulgent smile, noting that he had put on weight around the middle, and that there were one or two white hairs among the bristles of his red mustache. His blue eyes were innocent, almost childlike, and yet, Maigret remembered, he had been one of his ablest assistants.

"What are you smiling at?"

"Because I saw her alive, and yet you, who know her only from photographs and hearsay, have reached the same conclusions as I have."

"You mean that Hélène Lange was a prey to sentimental and romantic delusions?"

"I believe she was playing a part, deceiving even herself perhaps, but she couldn't hide the look in her eyes, which was hard and shrewd."

"Like her sister . . ."

"Francine Lange has cast herself in the role of the emancipated woman, who doesn't give a damn for anyone or anything. . . . If you were to ask in La Rochelle, I'm sure you'd find that she had a wide circle of friends, all of whom would regale you with colorful details of her conversations and escapades. . . ."

"Which is not to say . . ."

There was no need for either of them to spell things out.

"That, underneath it all, she doesn't know that two and two makes four!"

"And what's more, gigolos or no gigolos, she knows what she wants. . . . Starting with a miserable little shop in Marsilly, she now owns, at the age of forty, one of the smartest hairdressing salons in La Rochelle. I know the town. Place des Armes . . ."

He took out his pocket watch.

"My wife will be waiting. . . ."

"At the spring?"

"No, I'm going to watch a game or two of bowls first. It will give me something else to think about. . . . I used to play a bit years ago, at Porquerolles. If only some of those fellows would twist my arm . . ."

He went on his way, filling a fresh pipe. It was warmer than it had been. By the time he got there, he was glad of the shade of the great trees.

"Anything new?"

"Nothing of any interest."

"Haven't they found out about her life in Paris yet?"

His wife was eying him warily, not wishing to overstep the mark, but he answered with perfect good humor:

"Nothing definite. . . . Only that she had at least one lover."

Madame Maigret grew bolder.

"Anyone would think you were pleased!"

"In a way, perhaps. It shows that, for a time at least, she got a bit of fun out of life, that she wasn't always shut up inside herself, chewing over God knows what obsessions and fantasies. . . ."

"What do you know about him?"

"Practically nothing, except that he drove a big black car, and went to see her once or twice a week in the evening, and always left before ten.

They never went away together for a holiday, or even a weekend. . . ."

"A married man . . ."

"Probably. . . . Aged about forty, ten years older than she was. . . ."

"What about the neighbors in Rue du Bourbonnais? Did none of them ever see him?"

"Well, for one thing, he's not a man of forty now. More like sixty. . . ."

"Do you think . . . "

"I don't think anything. I'd like to know what sort of life she lived in Nice. Was it a period of transition, or had she already acquired the habits of an old maid? . . . Watch out, he's going to bowl. . . ."

The one-armed player, bowling with great deliberation, sent the jack spinning.

Involuntarily, he exclaimed:

"I envy them."

"Why?"

Her skin, dappled with sunlight and shade, was smooth. She's looking younger, he thought. His holiday mood was coming back. With a twinkle, he said:

"Haven't you noticed how completely engrossed they are? To them, bowling a good ball is the supreme fulfillment. It really is important to them. But when we come to the end of an inquiry . . ."

He left the sentence in the air, but his wry little grimace was eloquent. In this job, when they had finished with a man, he was abandoned, left to stand alone at the bar of Justice. . . . The end was prison, sometimes death. . . .

Shaking himself out of it, he emptied his pipe, and then said:

"What about our walk?"

Well, that was what they were here for, wasn't it?

Lecoeur's assistants had questioned all the neighbors.

Not only had no one heard or seen anything on the night of the murder, but all were agreed that Hélène Lange had no friends of either sex, and that she had never been known to have a visitor.

From time to time she was seen to leave the house carrying a small overnight bag, and on these occasions the shutters would remain closed for two or three days.

She never took any heavy luggage. She never ordered a taxi, and she had no car.

Nor had she ever been seen in the street with a companion, man or woman.

Every morning of the week, she went out to do her shopping in the local shops. Although she was not exactly mean, she knew the value of money, and on Saturdays always did her weekend shopping in the market. Invariably, she wore a hat, white in summer, dark in winter.

As to her present lodgers, they were completely in the clear. Madame Vireveau had come on the recommendation of a friend in Montmartre, who had stayed at Mademoiselle Lange's during the season, for several years in succession. A bit showy she might be, with her ample figure and flamboyant paste jewels, but she was not the woman to commit a murder, especially without motive. Her husband had been a florist in Paris, and up to the time of his death she had worked in the shop in Boulevard des Batignolles. Afterward she had moved to a little apartment in Rue La-marck.

"I had nothing against her," she said of Hé-lène Lange, "except that she had very little to say for herself."

The Maleskis had been coming to Vichy for the cure for the past four years. The first year, they had gone to a hotel, and had discovered Made-moiselle Lange quite by chance, through a card in a shop window advertising rooms to let, which they had noticed one day when they were out for a walk. They had inquired about her charges, and had at once booked a room for the following sea-son. This was their third summer at *Les Iris*.

Maleski suffered from a disease of the liver, which meant that he had to take care of himself and keep to a very strict diet. Although only for-ty-two, he was already burned out, a shadow of a man with a sad smile. Inquiries made over the telephone to Grenoble, however, revealed that he was at the top of his profession, and highly re-garded as a man of scrupulous honesty.

It had been made clear to him and his wife from the first that Mademoiselle Lange preferred to keep her distance with the lodgers. The only room they had ever been into on the ground floor was the little parlor, and then not more than two or three times. They had never been asked in for a drink, or even a cup of coffee.

Occasionally, when they stayed in on wet evenings, they could hear the television, but it was always turned off quite early.

All this information was buzzing in Maigret's head as he lay on the bed dozing, as he did every afternoon, while Madame Maigret sat at the window reading. Through half-closed eyes, he could see the lines of light thrown on the wall opposite the window by the slats of the Venetian blind, and was conscious of a golden afternoon outside.

Ideas swirled around and around in his head, broke up and reassembled, and suddenly he was asking himself, as though it were the key question:

"Why that night in particular?"

Why had she not been murdered the night before, or the night after, or last month, or two months ago?

On the face of it, it was a pointless question, and yet, half asleep as he was, he felt it to be of the utmost significance.

For ten years, ten long years, she had lived alone in that quiet Vichy street. No one had ever visited her. She, as far as anyone could tell, had never visited anyone, except perhaps when she was away on one of her brief monthly trips.

The neighbors had seen her as she came and went. She was also to be seen, sitting on one of the yellow chairs in the park, sipping her glass of water, or, in the evening near the bandstand, listening to the music.

Had Maigret personally questioned the shopkeepers, they would probably have been amazed at the things he wanted to know.

"Did she ever indulge in small talk? ... Did

you ever see her bend down and stroke your dog? Did she talk to the other housewives in the queue, or exchange greetings with those whom she regularly met at the same time, more or less every day?"

And finally:

"Have you ever known her to laugh? . . . Only smile?"

It was necessary to go back fifteen years to find evidence of any kind of personal relationship with another human being, the man who used to visit her once or twice a week in her apartment in Rue Notre-Dame-de-Lorette.

Was it possible that she could have lived all those years without ever feeling the need to unburden herself to anyone, to speak her thoughts aloud?

Someone had strangled her.

"But why that night in particular?"

To Maigret, half asleep as he was, this question was assuming obsessional proportions. He was still seeking an answer when his wife's voice broke in with the announcement that it was three o'clock.

"Were you asleep?"

"Dozing."

"Are we going out?"

"Of course we're going out! Don't we always go out? Why do you ask?"

"I thought you might be meeting Lecoeur."

"I'm not meeting anyone."

And, to prove it, he took her on a grand tour of the town, starting with the children's playground, and going on via the bowling greens and the beach, across the Pont de Bellerive, to walk the length of the boulevard leading to the Yacht Club, where they stopped for a while to watch the antics of the water skiers.

Then on much farther, as far as the new buildings, twelve stories high, towering white blocks that were, in themselves, a town on the outskirts of the town.

Across the Allier they could see the horses cantering alongside the white fence posts of the racecourse, and the heads and shoulders of the people in the stands, and, on the lawns, groups of figures in sunlight and in shadow.

"The proprietor of the hotel says that every year more and more retired people are coming to live in Vichy."

Teasingly, he asked:

"Is that what you're softening me up for?"

"We've got our house at Meung. . . ."

They came upon a street of older houses. Each district had its own style, representing its own period. The houses had their own individuality, and one could envisage the kind of people who had built them.

It amused Maigret to stop outside every one of the innumerable little restaurants they passed, and read the menu.

"Room to let. Room with kitchen. Luxurious furnished rooms."

That explained the restaurants, and also the tens of thousands of people streaming through the streets and along the promenades.

At five o'clock, at the spring, they were both glad to take the weight off their aching feet. They smiled understandingly at one another. Maybe

81

they had overdone it a bit. What were they trying to prove? That they were both young still?

In the crowd, they recognized two faces, those of "the happy pair," but there was something different about the way the man was looking at Maigret. What was more, instead of walking past, he was coming straight up to the Chief Superintendent, with his hand held out.

What could Maigret do, but take it?

"Don't you remember me?"

"I know I've seen you before, but I can't for the life of me recall . . ."

"Does the name Bébert mean anything to you?"

Nicknames like Bébert, P'tit Louis, and Grand Jules were common enough in his experience.

"The métro."

Smiling more broadly than ever, he turned to his wife, as if seeking confirmation.

"The first time you arrested me, it was during a procession in Boulevard des Capucines. . . . And, would you believe it, I can't even remember which Head of State it was in honor of, only the horse guards on either side of his carriage. . . . The second time was outside the entrance to the métro at the Bastille. You'd been following me for some time. . . . All this didn't happen yesterday. . . . I was a young man then. So, if I may say so, were you. . . ."

All Maigret could remember about the métro affair was that he had lost his hat while chasing the culprit across the Place de la Bastille, and good Lord, now he came to think of it, it had been a straw boater of the kind fashionable at the time—so this wasn't the first time he had worn a straw hat.

"How long were you sent down for?"

"Two years. . . . It taught me a lesson. . . . Made me pull myself together. To begin with, I worked for a junk dealer, mending vast quantities of old glass—I always was good with my hands."

He gave a knowing wink, intended, no doubt, to convey that this had been very useful to him in the days when he was a pickpocket.

"Then I met Madame."

He laid great emphasis on the "Madame," and quite glowed with pride as he spoke.

"No police record. She's always been straight. She was fresh from Brittany, working in a dairy. . . . It was never anything but serious with her, so we were married. . . . She even insisted on our going back home to her village for a real white wedding in church."

He exuded *joie de vivre* at every pore.

"I was almost sure it was you. . . . Every time I saw you . . . But I couldn't be quite certain . . . until this morning, when I opened my paper, and there was your photograph. . . ."

He pointed to the glasses in their little straw cases.

"Nothing serious, I hope?"

"I'm in excellent health."

"Me too, or so all the doctors say, but here I am all the same, on account of pains in the knee joints. . . . Hydrotherapy, massage under water, ultra-violet rays, the lot. . . . And you?"

"A few glasses of water."

"Oh, well, there can't be much wrong then. . . .

But I mustn't keep you and your good lady....
You played very fair with me in the old days....
Lovely weather, isn't it? ... Good day to you,
sir.... Say good-by, Bobonne...."

As he watched them disappear into the distance, Maigret was still smiling at the resolute
little ex-pickpocket's success story. Then his wife
saw the smile fade, and a worried frown take its
place. At length, with a sigh of relief, he said:

"I think I now know why ..."

"Why the woman was murdered?"

"No, why she was murdered on that particular
day.... Why she wasn't murdered last month or
last year...."

"What do you mean?"

"Ever since we got here we've been meeting the
same people two or three times a day, and have
come to know them quite well by sight.... Take
that nut case.... He's never spoken to me until
today, because he couldn't be sure about me until
he saw my picture in the paper....

"But then, this is the first time we've come for
the cure, and it will probably be the last. But if
we were to come back next year, we'd very likely
see quite a few familiar faces about the place.

"What I'm trying to say is this: there is someone else in Vichy who, like ourselves, is here for
the first time ... going through the same routine:
medical examination, tests, prescribed course of
treatment, visits to the springs, measured doses of
the waters to be taken at fixed hours....

"He must have seen Hélène Lange somewhere, and thought he recognized her.

"Then he saw her again, and again.... Maybe

he was not far from where she was sitting the other night, when she was listening to the music."

It all sounded so simple: Madame Maigret was surprised he should be making such a song and dance about it.

The Chief Superintendent, sensing this, hastened to add, not without a touch of self-mockery:

"According to the brochures, some two hundred thousand people come to Vichy every year for the cure. The season lasts six months, so presumably they pour in at the rate of more than thirty thousand a month. Assuming a third of them are newcomers like ourselves, that leaves us with about two thousand suspects. . . . No! Wait a bit . . . we can exclude the women and children. . . . What's the proportion of women and children, would you say?"

"There are more women than men. As to children . . ."

"No, wait! What about the people in wheel chairs, and those on crutches or walking with a stick? None of them, not to mention the very old, would be capable of strangling a healthy woman still in her prime. . . ."

Was he teasing her, or did he really mean it, she wondered.

"Let's say we're left with a thousand men capable of committing this murder. But, according to the evidence of Madame Vireveau and the proprietor of the bar, the murderer was unusually tall and thickset, so we can ignore the skinny and undersized . . . which leaves us with about five hundred."

It was a relief to hear him laugh.

"What's the joke?"

"The policeman's lot. Our job. I shall shortly inform the good Lecoeur that I have narrowed the field down to five hundred suspects, unless we are able to eliminate a few more, those who were at the theater that night, for instance, or who can prove that they spent the whole evening at the bridge tables, or what have you. . . . And to think that, more often than not, that's how criminals are caught! In one case, Scotland Yard questioned every single inhabitant of a town with a population of two hundred thousand. . . . It took months. . . ."

"Did they find their man?"

Wryly, Maigret had to admit:

"Quite by chance, in some other town. The fellow was drunk, and opened his mouth too wide."

It was probably too late to see Lecoeur today. There were still two glasses of water to be drunk, with a half-hour interval between. He tried to concentrate on the evening paper, which was full of gossip about visiting celebrities. It was an odd thing, but even those well known for the dissolute lives they led liked to be photographed surrounded by their children or grandchildren, asserting that they wanted nothing better than to spend all their time with them.

By the time they reached the corner of Rue d'Auvergne, there was a fresh breeze blowing. A truck was parked outside Mademoiselle Lange's house.

As they drew near, they could hear the sound of hammering.

"Shall I go back to the hotel?" murmured Madame Maigret.

"Yes. This won't take long."

The living-room door was open, and men in buff overalls were hanging black draperies on the walls.

Lecoeur came forward to meet him.

"I thought you might be coming. . . . We'll go in here. . . ."

Lecoeur led the way into the bedroom, where it was quieter.

"Is she to be buried in Vichy?" Maigret asked. "Is that what her sister has decided?"

"Yes, she was here just before lunch."

"With the gigolo?"

"No, she came alone in a taxi."

"When is the funeral?"

"The day after tomorrow, to give time for the neighbors to pay their last respects."

"Will there be prayers?"

"Apparently not."

"Are the Langes not Catholics?"

"The old people were. The children were baptized, and took their First Communion. After that . . ."

"I was wondering if she was divorced."

"To find the answer to that we should need to know whether she was ever married."

Lecoeur, twiddling the ends of his red mustache, looked inquiringly at Maigret.

"You yourself had never set eyes on either of them before, I take it?"

"Never."

"But you did spend some time in La Rochelle?"

"I've been there twice. . . . Each time, for about ten days. Why do you ask?"

"Because I noticed a change in Francine Lange this morning. She was a good deal less lively . . . less forthright. I had the feeling that she had something on her mind . . . that there was something she wanted to tell me, but she was of two minds about it. . . .

"At one point she said:

" 'Wasn't that Chief Superintendent Maigret who was here yesterday?'

"I asked her if she had ever seen you before, and she said no, but she had recognized your picture in the morning paper."

"She's not the only one. I suppose there must be about fifty others among the thousands I meet in the street every day. . . . Only today, an old customer of mine bore down on me with his hand outstretched. I was lucky to escape a hearty slap on the back."

"I think there's more to it than that," said Lecoeur, still following his own train of thought.

"You mean you think I may have had dealings with her when she was living in Paris?"

"Considering her mode of life, it's not all that far-fetched. . . . No! It's something less obvious, more subtle. . . . As far as she's concerned, I'm just a country cop, doing his best, asking the standard questions, noting the answers, and moving on to the next. . . . Do you see what I'm getting at? It would explain why, when she came here the first time, she was very much at her ease, as she was yesterday afternoon. . . . I caught her looking at you once or twice sitting there in the corner, but I could see she hadn't recognized you. . . .

"Then she booked in at the Hôtel de la Gare. There, as in most other hotels here, the local newspaper is sent up on the breakfast trays. . . . And when she saw your photograph, no doubt, she began to wonder what you were doing sitting in on our interview."

"And what are your conclusions?"

"Aren't you forgetting your reputation, your public image?"

He flushed suddenly, fearful that he might have given offense.

"Besides, it's not only the public. . . . We in the force are the first to . . ."

"Skip it. . . ."

"No, it's important. . . . It would never have crossed her mind that your presence—sitting in that armchair—might be fortuitous. . . . And even if it was, the very fact that you were interested in the case . . ."

"Did she seem at all frightened?"

"I wouldn't go as far as that. Her manner was different, more guarded. I only asked a few harmless questions, but even so, she weighed every word before answering. . . ."

"Has she traced the notary?"

"I wondered about that too. I did ask her. Apparently, the boy friend got a list of all the notaries in town, and rang every single one. . . . Hélène Lange, it seems, had never consulted any of them, though there was one who remembered that, ten years ago, when he was still an articled clerk, his firm had drawn up the deed of conveyance for her house."

"Do you know his name?"

"Maître Rambaud."

"What about giving him a ring?"

"At this hour?"

"Surely most lawyers outside Paris practice from their homes. . . ."

"What do you want me to ask him?"

"Whether she paid by check or bank draft."

"I'll have to stop those fellows' hammering first."

In the meantime, Maigret prowled back and forth from the bathroom to the kitchen, though not with anything particular in mind.

"Well?"

"You guessed, didn't you?"

"What?"

"That she paid in cash. It's the only time Rambaud has ever known it to happen, which is why he still remembers it. There were enough notes to fill a small suitcase."

"Have you taken statements from the ticket clerks at the railway station?"

"Good Lord! I never thought of that!"

"It would be interesting to find out whether she always went to the same place on her monthly trips, or to a different place each time. . . ."

"I'll let you know tomorrow. . . . It's time you were off to your dinner. . . . Enjoy yourself! . . ."

There was a band concert in the park that night, and the Maigrets permitted themselves the luxury of sitting down to listen to it. They had walked far enough for one day.

4

For some mysterious reason, he was ten minutes ahead of schedule. Maybe there was less news than usual in this morning's *Journal de Clermont-Ferrand*? Madame Maigret, who always waited until he had finished before going into the bathroom, was still in there. He called to her through the half-open door:

"I'm going out. . . . Wait for me downstairs."

There was a green wooden seat on the sidewalk outside the hotel, for the convenience of residents. The sky was as cloudless as ever. During the whole of their stay in Vichy, it had not rained once.

Needless to say, the proprietor was waiting for him at the foot of the stairs.

"Well, what news of the murder?"

"It's no concern of mine," he answered with a smile.

"Do you think that these Clermont-Ferrand people are really up to the job? It's very bad, in a place like this, to have a strangler on the loose.

Quite a number of old ladies have left already, I hear. . . ."

With a noncommittal smile, he set off for Rue du Bourbonnais. He saw, from the far end of the street, that the front door of *Les Iris* was draped in black, with a large letter "L" embroidered in silver on the pelmet. There was no longer a policeman on guard outside. Had there been one last night? He had not noticed. After all, it was none of his business. He was here to take the waters, and his only interest in the case was as a bystander, an amateur.

He was about to ring the bell when he noticed that the white door was ajar. He pushed it open and went in. A very young girl, barely sixteen, he judged, was mopping the floor of the entrance with a damp cloth. Her dress was so short that, when she bent forward, he could see her pink bloomers. She had plump, shapeless legs, as girls so often do at the awkward age. They reminded him of the crudely painted legs of a cheap doll.

She turned to look at him, a pair of expressionless eyes staring at him out of a round face. She did not ask his name, nor what he was doing there.

"In there," was all she said, pointing to the living room.

The room, all draped in black, was dark, with the coffin resting on what must have been the dining-room table. There were unlit candles, holy water in a glass bowl, and a sprig of rosemary.

The kitchen and dining-room doors were open. The living-room furniture and ornaments had been stacked in the dining room. The young policeman, Dicelle, was sitting in the kitchen reading a comic, with a cup of coffee on the table in front of him.

"Will you join me in a cup of coffee? I've made a full pot."

On Hélène Lange's gas cooker, which would scarcely have met with her approval!

"Hasn't Superintendent Lecoeur arrived yet?"

"He was called back urgently to Clermont-Ferrand late last night. . . . A holdup at the Savings Bank. . . . One man killed . . . a passer-by, who noticed the door ajar and went in to investigate, just as the thieves were coming out. . . . One of them shot him at point-blank range. . . ."

"Nothing new here?"

"Not that I know of."

"Have you questioned the station staff?"

"Trigaud—one of my colleagues—is looking into it. He's not back yet."

"I presume the little servant-girl out there has been questioned? What has she to say?"

"That half-wit! It's a wonder she can talk at all! She doesn't know a thing. She was only taken on for the season, to see to the lodgers' rooms. She didn't do the ground floor; Mademoiselle Lange saw to her own housework."

"Did she ever see any visitors?"

"Only the man who reads the gas meter, and the delivery boys. She came to work at nine and left at twelve. . . . The Maleskis upstairs are a bit worried. . . . They've paid in advance to the end of the month, and they want to know whether they'll be able to stay on. . . . It isn't easy to find rooms in the middle of the season, and they don't want to move to a hotel."

"What does the Superintendent say?"

"I think, as far as he's concerned, they can stay.... They're up there now, at any rate.... The other one, the fat one, has gone to the masseur for her daily pummeling."

"Have you seen Francine Lange?"

"I'm expecting her any time.... No one seems to know what's happening.... She insisted on the lying-in-state, but it wouldn't surprise me if no one turned up.... My instructions are to stay here and keep a discreet eye on the callers, if any."

"I wish you joy of it," mumbled Maigret, going out of the kitchen.

The books, like everything else from the living room, had been moved into the dining room. Mechanically, he picked one up off the top of a pile stacked on a small occasional table. It was *Lucien Leuwen*. The yellowing pages had the distinctive smell of well-thumbed books from lending libraries, public or private.

The name and address of the library was stamped in violet ink on the flyleaf.

He put the book back on top of the pile and slipped quietly out into the street. A ground-floor window opened, and a woman in a dressing gown and hair-rollers looked out.

"Excuse me, Superintendent, can you tell me if one can call and pay one's respects?"

It seemed to him rather an odd way of putting it, and for a moment he was nonplused.

"I imagine so. The door is open, and they've turned the living room into a little chapel."

"Can one see her?"

"As far as I know, the coffin is closed."

She sighed:

"I prefer it that way. . . . It's less distressing."

He found Madame Maigret waiting for him on the green seat. She seemed surprised to see him back so soon.

They set off on their usual morning walk. They were only a couple of minutes behind schedule, a schedule that they had never planned, but now adhered to as though their lives depended on it.

"Were there many people?"

"Not a soul. They're waiting. . . ."

This time they went straight to the children's playground, where they strolled for a time in the shade of the trees, some of which—like those along the banks of the Allier—were very rare specimens, from America, India, and Japan. These were distinguished by little metal plates, bearing their botanical names in Latin and French. Many were tokens of gratitude from long-forgotten Heads of State, who had benefited from the cure at Vichy, obscure maharajahs and other Eastern princelings.

They did not stop more than a minute or two at the bowling greens. Madame Maigret never asked her husband where they were making for. He always walked purposefully, as though he knew exactly where he was going, but more often than not he would turn down this street rather than that, just for a change of scene, because he enjoyed savoring new sights and sounds.

They still had a little time in hand before the first glass of water, when he turned into Rue Georges-Clemenceau. Was there something he wanted from the shops, she wondered? But he turned left into one of the little side alleys, the one leading to the theater, and stopped at a bookshop, where there were some second-hand books in trays on the sidewalk, and more books inside on revolving shelves.

"Come on," he said to his wife, who was looking at him inquiringly.

The proprietor, in a long gray overall, was tidying the shelves. He obviously recognized Maigret, but waited for him to speak.

"Can you spare me a few minutes?"

"With pleasure, Monsieur Maigret. It's about Mademoiselle Lange, I daresay."

"She was one of your subscribers, wasn't she?"

"She came in at least once a week, twice more often than not, to change her books. Her subscription allowed her to have two books out at a time."

"How long have you known her?"

"I took over here six years ago. I'm not a local man. I came here from Paris, Montparnasse. She was already a subscriber in my predecessor's time."

"Did she ever stop for a chat?"

"Well, you know, she wasn't very outgoing...."

"Didn't she ever ask your advice, when she was choosing new books?"

"She had very decided views of her own. Come with me...."

He led the way to a room at the back of the

shop, lined from floor to ceiling with books in black cloth bindings.

"She would often spend half an hour to an hour browsing in here, reading a paragraph here and a page there."

"Her last book was Stendhal's *Lucien Leuwen*."

"Stendhal was her latest discovery. Before that, she had read all Chateaubriand, Alfred de Vigny, Jules Sandeau, Benjamin Constant, Musset, and George Sand. It was always the romantics. On one occasion she took one of Balzac's novels—I can't remember which—but she brought it back the next day. Apparently it didn't appeal to her. I asked her why. She said: 'It's too coarse ...' or words to that effect. . . . Balzac coarse, I ask you!"

"No contemporary writers?"

"She never gave them a chance. On the other hand, she read the letters of George Sand and Musset over and over again."

"I'm much obliged to you. . . ."

He was almost at the door when the bookseller called him back.

"Just one more thing that might interest you. I discovered, to my astonishment, that someone had been marking passages in pencil, underlining words and phrases and, here and there, putting a cross in the margin. I wondered who on earth it could be. It turned out in the end to be Mademoiselle Lange."

"Did you mention it to her?"

"I had to. . . . My assistant was having to spend all his time rubbing out the marks. . . ."

"How did she react?"

"She looked very prim and said 'I'm sorry. . . .

When I'm reading I forget that the books don't belong to me.'"

Everything looked just the same, the people taking the waters, the pale trunks of the plane trees, the patches of sun and shade, the thousands of yellow chairs.

She had not been able to stomach Balzac....

His realism had been too much for her, no doubt. She had restricted herself to the first half of the nineteenth century, grandly dismissing Flaubert, Hugo, Zola, Maupassant.... At the same time Maigret had noticed, that very first day, a pile of glossy magazines in a corner of the living room....

It was as though he could not help himself, he must forever be adding fresh touches to the picture of her that he was building up. Her reading was confined to the romantic, the sentimental, and yet he had more than once seen her eyes narrow in a hard, shrewd look.

"Did you see Lecoeur?"

"No. He's been called back to Clermont-Ferrand because of a bank holdup."

"Do you think he'll find the murderer?"

Maigret started. He was the one who needed bringing down to earth! The truth was that he had not been thinking about the case in terms of murder. He had almost forgotten that the woman who owned the house with the green shutters had been strangled, and that the first priority was to find the killer.

True, he was looking for someone, more intensely, indeed, than he himself would have wished, almost to the point where it was becoming an obsession.

The really intriguing figure, as far as he was concerned, was the man who, at a given moment, had broken into the life of this solitary woman.

There was no trace of him in Rue du Bourbonnais, no photograph, not a single letter, not even a note.

Nothing! Nothing from anyone else either, apart from bills and receipts.

One had to go back twelve years, to Paris, to Rue Notre-Dame-de-Lorette, to find anyone who remembered a shadowy figure who called once or twice a week, and spent an hour in the apartment of Mademoiselle Lange, then still a comparatively young woman.

Even Francine, her own sister, who was living in the same city at the time, claimed to know nothing about him.

She read voraciously, watched television, did her shopping and her housework, walked under the trees in the park like the summer visitors, sat and listened to the band, staring straight in front of her, and never addressing a word to anyone.

This was what puzzled him. Often, in the course of his career, he had met individuals, both men and women, who clung fiercely to their independence. He had also met eccentrics who, having renounced the world, had taken refuge in the most unlikely, sometimes the most sordid, surroundings.

But even men and women such as these, in his experience, kept some link with the outside world. The old ones, for instance, often had a favorite bench in a square, where they would meet some other old crone to talk to, or they were members of a church, going to confession, exchanging greetings with the priest. Some had a favorite bistro, where they were known, and welcomed as old friends.

But here was a case, Maigret realized—the first he had ever known—of stark, unrelieved isolation.

There was not even an element of aggression. Mademoiselle Lange had been civil enough to the neighbors and shopkeepers. She had not been high-handed with them nor, in spite of her somewhat formal style of dress and her preference for certain colors, had she put on superior airs.

It was rather that she did not concern herself with other people. She had no need of them. She took in lodgers because the spare bedrooms were there, and they provided a small income. Between the apartment on the ground floor and the bedrooms upstairs, she had erected an invisible barrier, and to clean the guest rooms she had engaged a servant girl, who was little better than a moron.

"Can you spare a moment, sir?"

A shadow fell across Maigret. He looked up to see a tall man holding a chair by its back. The Chief Superintendent recognized him as one of the men he had seen with Dicelle in Rue du Bourbonnais, Trigaud presumably.

"How did you find me?" Maigret asked.

"Dicelle said you would be here."

"And how did Dicelle . . . ?"

"There isn't a man in the local force, sir, who

doesn't know you by sight, so that wherever you go . . ."

"Any fresh news?"

"I was at the station for an hour last night, interviewing the night staff, and this morning I went back to question the day staff. . . . Then I called Superintendent Lecoeur, who is still at Clermont-Ferrand. . . ."

"Won't he be back today?"

"He's not sure yet. But whatever happens, he'll be coming early tomorrow for the funeral. I presume you'll be there, too. . . ."

"Have you seen Francine?"

"She called in at the undertaker's. The hearse will be leaving the house at nine o'clock. . . . Some flowers were delivered at the house. . . . They must have come from her, I imagine. . . ."

"How many wreaths?"

"Just the one."

"Check whether it did come from her. . . . I beg your pardon. . . . I was forgetting . . . it's really none of my business."

"I don't think the Super would agree with you there. He told me to be sure and let you know what I'd found out. He made a special point of it. I expect that there are a good many in the force, including your humble servant, who would go along with that. . . ."

"On these monthly trips of hers, did she go far?"

Trigaud pulled a bundle of papers out of his pocket and, after some searching, found what he was looking for.

"They couldn't remember all the details, of

course, but one or two places stuck in their minds, because they are by no means easy to get to from here: Strasbourg, for instance, and the following month, Brest. Some of her trips involved changing trains two or three times: Carcassonne ... Dieppe ... Lyons ... not quite so far ... Lyons was, in fact, exceptional.... Mostly, she went much farther afield: Nancy, Montélimar."

"Never to a small town or a village?"

"No, she always seemed to choose a fairly large town, though, of course, she may have gone on somewhere by bus."

"Did she never take a ticket to Paris?"

"Never."

"How long has this been going on?"

"The last man I spoke to has been working at the same window for nine years.

"'I ought to know my regular customers by now,' he said.

"She was well known to the station staff. They looked forward to her coming, and even laid bets as to where she would choose to go next."

"Did she always go on the same day of the month?"

"No, that's the odd thing. Sometimes there would be an interval of six weeks, usually in the summer. I daresay it was on account of the lodgers. It wasn't always the end of the month, or any fixed date."

"Did Lecoeur tell you what he intends to do next?"

"He's having copies made of her photographs. ... For a start, he'll send a couple of men to the nearest towns, and copies of the photographs to the various local police stations. . . ."

"You don't happen to know why Lecoeur wanted me put in the picture?"

"He didn't say. . . . No doubt he thought you had formed your own view. . . . That's what I think, too. . . ."

Everyone always credited him with knowing more than he let on. It was no good protesting. They would only think it was the old fox up to his usual tricks.

"Has anyone turned up at the house?"

"According to Dicelle, things started livening up around ten o'clock. . . . A woman in an apron put her head around the door, and then, rather hesitantly, went in to see the coffin. She took a rosary out of her pocket and muttered a prayer. Then she crossed herself with holy water and left. . . .

"She must have told the neighbors, because they all came after that, in ones and twos. . . ."

"Any men?"

"A few . . . . the butcher, and a carpenter who lives at the end of the street . . . all local people. . . ."

Why assume that the murderer wasn't a local man? They were searching up and down the country, in all the widely separated towns visited by the lady in lilac, in Nice, in Paris, trying to unravel the mystery of her life. But no one had given a thought to the thousands of people who lived in the France district of Vichy.

Maigret himself had not.

"Can you suggest anything further I should do?"

Trigaud wasn't saying this on his own. That cunning devil Lecoeur must have put him up to it. After all, here was Maigret on the spot. Why not make use of him?

"I was wondering whether the ticket clerks could remember any precise dates. We wouldn't need very many. Two or three would do."

"I have one already.... June 11th.... The fellow remembered it because she took a ticket for Rheims, and his wife comes from there, and, as it happened, June 11th was her birthday."

"If I were you, I'd find out from her bank manager whether she deposited any money on the 13th or 14th...."

"I think I see what you're driving at ... blackmail."

"Or an allowance ..."

"Why should anyone pay out an allowance at irregular intervals?"

"Just what I was wondering myself."

Trigaud stole a sideways glance at Maigret, convinced that he was either keeping something from him or making fun of him.

"I'd much rather they'd put me on the holdup," he grumbled. "At least you know where you stand with pros.... I'm sorry to have bothered you.... My best respects, madame."

He got up awkwardly, not quite knowing how to make his escape, blinking, with the sun full in his eyes.

"It's too late now for the bank. I'll call in there

after lunch. Then, if necessary, I'll go back to the railway station."

Maigret had been through it all in his time. Pounding the beat for hours at a stretch, on pavements scorching hot or slippery with rain, questioning wary witnesses, whose words had to be coaxed out of them, one by one.

"We'd better go and have our glass of water."

While Trigaud, no doubt, would be regaling himself with a long, cool glass of beer.

"You'd better be at the spring at about eleven. . . . I hope I'll be able to get there."

He sounded a little out of temper. Madame Maigret had been afraid that he would get bored in Vichy, with nothing to do, and no one but herself for company, from morning to night.

The good-humored contentment that he had shown in the first few days had not wholly reassured her. She could not help wondering how long it would last.

However, in the past two or three days, he had been thoroughly put out every time they had had to miss one of their regular walks.

Today there was the funeral. He had promised Lecoeur to be there. The sun was still shining, and, as usual in the morning, the streets were damp, and a fresh breeze was blowing.

Rue du Bourbonnais was unusually crowded. Apart from the neighbors who could be seen leaning out of their windows, like spectators at a public procession, there were people all along the sidewalk several deep outside the house itself.

The hearse was already there. Behind it was a

black car supplied, no doubt, by the undertaker, and behind that another, which Maigret had not seen before.

Lecoeur came out to meet him.

"I've had to drop the bank robbery for the time being," he explained. "There's a holdup practically every day of the week. The public are used to them, and they don't get het up about them any more. But a woman strangled in her own house, in a law-abiding town like Vichy, and for no apparent reason . . ."

Maigret recognized the scruffy mop of red hair belonging to the *Tribune* photographer. There were two or three other photographers there as well. One of them took a shot of the two police officers crossing the road.

The fact was that there was nothing to see, and, from the expressions on their faces, some of the bystanders were wondering whether it had really been worth their while to come.

"Have you got men on watch in the street?"

"Three. . . . . I can't see Dicelle, but he's somewhere around. . . . He thought it would be a good idea to have the butcher's boy with him. . . . He knows everyone hereabouts, and will be able to point out any strangers."

There was no feeling of sadness, no sense of horror. Everyone, Maigret included, was waiting.

"Will you be going to the cemetery?" he asked Lecoeur.

"I'd be glad if you'd come with me, Chief. I've brought my own car. I felt a police car wouldn't be quite the thing. . . ."

"What about Francine?"

"She got here a few minutes ago, with the boy friend. . . . They're in the house."

"I don't see their car."

"I daresay the undertakers, who know what's what, dropped a hint that an open red sports job would look just as much out of place in a funeral procession as a police car. . . . Those two will go in the black car."

"Have you spoken to her?"

"She gave me a nod when she arrived. I thought she looked nervous . . . anxious. . . . She stood for a moment, before coming into the house, scanning the crowd as though she was looking for someone. . . ."

"I still can't see young Dicelle."

"That's because he's wangled a seat in someone's window, for himself and the butcher's boy."

Several people came out of the house, two more went in and reappeared almost at once. Then the driver of the hearse took his seat at the wheel.

As though in response to a signal, four men, not without difficulty, maneuvered the coffin through the door and slid it into the hearse. One of them went back into the house and returned carrying a wreath and a small spray of flowers.

"The spray is from the lodgers."

Francine Lange stood at the door, in a black dress that did not suit her. She must have bought it for the occasion in Rue Georges-Clemenceau. Her companion was behind her, a shadowy figure in the darkness of the entrance hall.

The hearse moved forward a few feet. Francine and her lover got into the black car.

"Let's go, Chief."

All along the street there were people, standing very still. Only the photographers were darting hither and thither.

"Is that all ?" Maigret asked, looking over his shoulder.

"She had no other relatives . . . no friends. . . ."

"What about the lodgers?"

"Maleski is seeing his doctor at ten, and the fat woman, Madame Vireveau, has her massage. . . ."

They drove through streets that Maigret recognized from his exploration of the town. He filled his pipe, and watched the houses go by. Soon, to his surprise, they were at the railway station.

The cemetery was nearby, just on the other side of the track. It was deserted. The hearse stopped at the end of the drive.

So here they were, just the four of them, except for the undertaker's men, standing on the gravel path. Lecoeur and Maigret went up to the other two. The gigolo was wearing sunglasses.

"Will you be staying long?" Maigret asked the young woman.

Maigret had spoken idly, just for something to say, but it did not escape him that she was looking penetratingly at him, as though searching for some hidden meaning in his words.

"Probably another two or three days, just to get things sorted out."

"What about the lodgers?"

"They can stay till the end of the month. There's no reason why not. I'll just have to lock up the ground-floor apartment."

"Will you be selling the house?"

Before she could answer, one of the men in

black came up to her. They wheeled the coffin, on a handcart, down a narrow side turning to the edge of an open grave.

A photographer—not the tall, redheaded man, but another whom Maigret had not seen before—appeared, apparently from nowhere, and took a few shots while the coffin was being lowered into the grave, then another as Francine, at a sign from the master of ceremonies, threw a handful of earth onto the coffin.

The grave was at the far end of the cemetery, a few yards from the low surrounding wall which divided it from a patch of waste ground, where derelict cars lay rotting. Beyond, in the background, were one or two white villas.

The hearse drove away, then the photographer. Lecoeur looked inquiringly at Maigret, who, however, did not respond, and seemed to be lost in thought. What precisely was he thinking of? Of La Rochelle, a town he had always liked, of Rue Notre-Dame-de-Lorette, as it was in the very early days when he was personal assistant to the Superintendent of Police in the IXth *Arrondissement*, of the bowling greens, and the men he had seen there. . . .

Francine, clutching a crumpled handkerchief, was coming toward them. She had not used the handkerchief to dry her tears. She had not shed a tear. She had been no more moved than the undertaker's men or the gravedigger. Indeed, there had been nothing in the least moving about the ceremony. It could not have been more matter-of-fact.

The crumpled handkerchief was just for the sake of appearances.

"I don't know the form. . . . It's usual, isn't it, to provide refreshments of some sort after a funeral? But I'm sure you wouldn't want to have lunch with us. . . ."

"There's so much to be done," murmured Lecoeur.

"At least allow me to buy you a drink."

Maigret was astonished at the change in her. Even here, in this desert of a cemetery, from which even the photographer had fled, she was still looking about her anxiously, as though she felt some danger threatening her.

"I'm sure there will be other opportunities," replied Lecoeur diplomatically.

"Haven't you got a lead yet?"

It was not at Lecoeur that she looked as she spoke, but at Chief Superintendent Maigret, as though he were the one she was afraid of.

"We're still making inquiries."

Maigret filled his pipe, and pressed down the tobacco with his forefinger. He was puzzled. This was a woman who had certainly had a few knocks in her time, and was quite capable of taking things in her stride. It was not her sister's death that had changed her. She had been cheerful and ebullient enough when she had first heard of it.

"In that case, gentlemen . . . I don't know how to put it. . . . Oh, well, I daresay I'll be seeing you. . . . Thanks for coming."

If she had waited a minute or two longer, Maigret might have asked her point-blank whether she had received any threats. But she went, teetering on her high heels, impatient to get back to her hotel room, where she could shut the door and change out of the black dress, bought especially for the occasion.

Maigret turned to his colleague from Clermont-Ferrand.

"What do you make of her?" he asked.

"So you noticed it, too? I'd very much like a private chat with her in my office. But I'd have to find a plausible excuse. It wouldn't be decent today, somehow. . . . She looked scared, to me."

"That was what I thought."

"Do you think she's been threatened? What would you do, if you were I?"

"What do you mean?"

"We don't know why her sister was strangled. . . . It might, after all, turn out to be a family affair. . . . We know precious little about these people. . . . Maybe it was some business in which both women were concerned. . . . Didn't I hear her tell you she'd be staying on in Vichy for another two or three days? I'm short-handed, of course, but the holdup can wait. . . . The pros always get caught in the end. . . ."

They had returned to their car and were driving toward the cemetery gates.

"I shall have her followed, discreetly, though in a hotel that's almost impossible. . . . Where would you like me to drop you?"

"Anywhere near the park."

"Ah, yes, I'd almost forgotten you were here for the cure. . . . I don't know why I've never got around to taking it myself. . . ."

At first he thought his wife had not yet arrived. She wasn't sitting in her usual place. He was so used to seeing her there that it gave him quite a start when he found her sitting in the shade, under a different tree.

For a moment he watched her, unseen. Sitting there placidly, with her hands folded in the lap of her light dress, she was looking at the people passing by, with a contented little smile, as though she were quite prepared to wait for him forever.

"Oh, there you are!" she exclaimed, then, without pausing, "Our chairs were taken. . . . I heard them talking. . . . They're Dutch, I think. . . . I hope they're not staying . . . otherwise we've probably lost our seats for good. . . . I didn't think it would be over so soon. . . ."

"It's not far to the cemetery."

"Were there many people?"

"In the street outside the house. . . . There were only the four of us at the funeral."

"So the boy friend went too, did he? Come on, it's time for our glass of water. . . ."

They had to wait in a queue for a time. Afterward, Maigret bought the Paris newspapers, but there was scarcely a mention of the Vichy strangler. One paper only, the evening paper of the previous day, had a photograph of Maigret under a headline in those very words: "The Vichy Strangler."

He was anxious to hear what, if anything, had been discovered as a result of the inquiries made in several of the many towns visited at various times by the lady in lilac.

Nevertheless, he allowed his mind to wander.

With half an eye on the news, he could see the people walking past, over the top of his paper. After a time, they had to push their chairs back into the receding shade.

That was why they had chosen the place now occupied by the Dutch couple. The sun never reached it at the times they were in the park.

"Don't you want a paper?"

"No. . . . Those two comics have just gone by, and he swept you a tremendous bow."

They were already lost in the crowd.

"Did the sister cry?"

"No."

He was still puzzled by her. If he had been in charge of the case, he too would have wanted to have her in his office for a private chat.

Several times, in the course of the morning, his thoughts returned to her. They walked back to the Hôtel de la Bérézina and, after going upstairs to wash, sat down at their table in the dining room. As usual, at every table except theirs, there were opened wine bottles beside the little trumpet-shaped vases, each holding one or two fresh flowers.

"There's cutlet Milanaise and calves' liver *à la bourgeoise.* . . ."

"I'll have the cutlet," he said with a sigh. "It will be grilled as usual, of course. I'll be gone by the end of the season, but Rian will still be here next year and the year after. What he says goes. . . ."

"Don't you feel the better for it?"

"Only because I'm away from Paris. Besides, I never felt really ill. A bit weighed down . . . giddiness from time to time. . . . These things happen to most people some time or other, I imagine."

"Still, you do have faith in Pardon. . . ."

"I haven't much choice."

They had had noodles as a first course and were just starting on their cutlets when Maigret was called to the telephone.

The telephone booth was in one of the smaller reception rooms, with a window overlooking the street.

"Hello! I'm not disturbing you, I hope? Had you started your lunch?"

Recognizing Lecoeur's voice, he replied crossly:

"For all they give me to eat!"

"I have news for you. . . . I sent one of my men to keep watch on the Hôtel de la Gare. . . . But first he thought he'd better find out the number of Francine Lange's room. The receptionist looked surprised, and told him she'd checked out. . . ."

"When?"

"Barely half an hour after they left us. It seems that, when they got back to the hotel, the man stopped at the desk before going up to their room, and asked them to get their bill ready. They must have packed in a great hurry, because ten minutes later they rang for a porter. They flung everything into the back of the red car, and off they went."

Maigret said nothing, and Lecoeur did not prompt him. After an appreciable pause, Lecoeur said:

"What do you make of it, Chief?"

"She's a frightened woman. . . ."

"Agreed, but she was this morning, too, anyone

could see that. . . . But that didn't prevent her from saying she intended staying another two or three days in Vichy."

"That might have been just to prevent you from detaining her."

"How could I detain her, not having anything against her?"

"You know the law, but she may not."

"Anyway, we shall know tomorrow morning, if not tonight, whether she's gone back to La Rochelle."

"It's the most likely thing."

"I agree. I'm furious, all the same. I'd made up my mind that we were going to have a long chat. . . . Admittedly, I may find out more, as a result of this. . . . Could you be here at two?"

It would mean missing his afternoon rest. He said, rather grudgingly:

"I'm not doing anything in particular, as you very well know."

"This morning, while I was out, someone phoned the local Police Station asking to speak to me. . . . That's where I am now. . . . I decided, after all, to take them up on their offer of a room here. . . . The caller was a young woman, apparently by the name of Madeleine Dubois, and guess what she does for a living. . . ."

Maigret said nothing.

"She's a switchboard operator on the night shift at the Hôtel da la Gare. My colleague here told her that I would probably be here at the station—it's in Avenue Victoria—at two o'clock. . . . He suggested that she should leave a message, but she said she'd prefer to see me personally.... So I'm here, waiting for her...."

"I'll be there."

He missed his rest but, by way of compensation, had the pleasure of seeing for the first time the exquisite, white turreted villa set in extensive grounds which did duty as a police station in Vichy. He was taken to the upper floor by a policeman and, at the end of a corridor, found Lecoeur ensconced in an office almost entirely devoid of furniture.

"It's just five to two," remarked Lecoeur. "I hope she hasn't changed her mind. Which reminds me, I'd better try and find another chair."

Maigret could hear him in the hall opening and shutting doors. Eventually he found what he wanted, and came back carrying it.

On the dot of two, the police officer on duty knocked at the door and announced:

"Madame Dubois."

She was a lively little woman, with dark hair and very expressive eyes. She stood there, looking from one to the other.

"Which of you is the officer I have come to see?"

Lecoeur introduced himself but not Maigret, who was sitting unobtrusively in a corner of the room.

"I don't know whether what I have to tell you is important.... It didn't seem so at the time.... The hotel is full, and I was kept very busy until one in the morning.... After that I dozed off, as I usually do.... It's about one of the hotel guests, Madame Lange...."

"I presume you mean Mademoiselle Francine Lange?"

"I thought she was married. I know her sister is dead, and that her funeral was this morning. . . . Last evening, at about half past eight, someone asked to speak to her. . . ."

"A man?"

"Yes, a man. He had an odd sort of voice. . . . Asthmatic, I think . . . I'm almost sure. . . . I had an uncle who suffered from asthma, and he sounded just like that. . . ."

"Did he give his name?"

"No."

"Did he ask for her room number?"

"No. I rang, and there was no reply . . . so I told him that the person he wanted to speak to was out. . . . He called again at about nine, but there was still no reply from Room 406. . . ."

"Did Mademoiselle Lange and her companion share a double room?"

"Yes. . . . The man phoned the third time at eleven, and this time Mademoiselle Lange answered. . . . I put him through. . . ."

She seemed embarrassed, and glanced quickly at Maigret, as though trying to gauge his reactions. Presumably she, like everyone else, had recognized him.

"Did you listen?" murmured Lecoeur, with an encouraging smile.

"I'm afraid I did. . . . I don't make a habit of it. . . . I know everyone imagines switchboard girls are always listening to people's conversations. If they only knew how boring they were, they'd think differently. . . . Perhaps it was because of the murder of her sister ... Or because the man had such a peculiar voice ...

" 'Who's speaking?' she said.

" 'Is that Mademoiselle Francine Lange?'

" 'Yes. ...'

" 'Are you alone?'

"She hesitated. ... I'm almost sure the man was in there with her.

" 'Yes,' she said, 'but what business is it of yours?'

" 'I have something very private to tell you. ... Listen carefully. ... If I'm interrupted, I shall call back in half an hour. ...'

"He had difficulty with his breathing, and every now and again he wheezed, just like my uncle.

" 'I'm listening ... you still haven't told me who you are. ...'

" 'It's of no importance. ... What is of the utmost importance—what is essential—is that you should stay on in Vichy for a few days. ... It's in your own interest. ... I'll be in touch with you again. ... I can't say when exactly. ... There may be a great deal in it for you. ... a large sum of money. ... Do you understand?'

"Then suddenly he stopped speaking, and hung up. A few minutes later a call came through from Room 406.

" 'Mademoiselle Lange here. ... I've just had a phone call. ... Could you tell me whether it was a local or a long-distance call?'

" 'Local.'

" 'Thank you!'

"Well, that's it! At first I thought it wasn't any business of mine. But when I came off duty this

118

morning, I just couldn't get to sleep, so I phoned here and asked to speak to the officer in charge of the case."

She was fidgeting nervously with her handbag, her glance shifting from one man to the other.

"Do you think it's important?"

"You haven't been back to the hotel?"

"I don't go on duty until eight o'clock in the evening."

"Mademoiselle Lange has left."

"Wasn't she at her sister's funeral?"

"She left almost immediately after the funeral."

"Oh!"

Then, after a pause for thought:

"You think the man was setting a trap for her, don't you? Could it, by any chance, have been the strangler?"

The color drained from her face at the thought that she had actually heard the voice of the lady in lilac's murderer.

Maigret was no longer regretting having missed his afternoon rest.

5

The two men stayed where they were after the telephone girl had left, Maigret puffing reflectively at his pipe, and Lecoeur smoking a cigarette that looked as if it were going to set fire to his mustache at any minute. The smoke rose, spread out, and hung above their heads. Down below in the yard, they could hear a squad of policemen drilling.

For a time, neither spoke. They were both old hands, and there was little anyone could teach them about their trade. They had had dealings with every sort of criminal, every sort of witness.

"There's no doubt that it was he calling her," Lecoeur said at last, with a sigh.

Maigret did not reply at once. His reaction was different. It wasn't so much a question of method—a term they both disliked—as of approach to a problem.

Thus, since the strangling of the lady in lilac, Maigret had given very little thought to the murderer. It was not deliberate, but simply because he was haunted by the recollection of this wom-

an, sitting on her yellow chair near the bandstand, haunted by the memory of her long jaw
line, and by her gentle smile, which belied the
hard expression of her eyes.

Little details had been added to his picture of
her as a result of his visits to her house in Rue du
Bourbonnais. He had learned something, though
not much, of her stay in Nice, her life in Paris,
and a great deal about her taste in literature.

The strangler was still a very shadowy figure, a
tall, heavily built man, whom Madame Vireveau
claimed to have seen, walking very rapidly, at the
corner of the street, and who had been glimpsed
by the proprietor of a bar, who could not describe
his features.

Almost without realizing it, he began thinking
about him.

"I wonder how he found out that Francine
Lange was staying at the Hôtel de la Gare."

The newspapers, which had announced the arrival in Vichy of the victim's sister, had given no
address.

Maigret was feeling his way forward cautiously, one step at a time.

"Come to think of it, there was nothing to prevent him from ringing one hotel after another,
and asking for Mademoiselle Lange."

He could picture him poring over a classified
directory. The list of hotels in a place like this
would be a long one. Had he gone through it in
alphabetical order?

"You might try one of the hotels beginning with
the letter 'A' or 'B.'"

With a twinkle in his eye, Lecoeur picked up the receiver.

"Get me the Hôtel d'Angleterre, will you? No, not the manager or the desk—I want the switchboard operator. Hello! Is that the switchboard of the Hôtel d'Angleterre? I'm a police officer. . . . Can you tell me if anyone has been asking to speak to Mademoiselle Lange? . . . No, not the murdered woman. . . . Her sister, Francine Lange. . . . That's right. . . . Perhaps your colleague would know. . . ."

He turned to Maigret:

"There are two girls on the switchboard. . . . It's a huge place. . . . Five or six hundred rooms. . . . Hello, yes. . . . Hello! You say you took the call yourself? . . . Anything strike you as odd? . . . A hoarse voice, did you say? . . . As though the man . . . Yes, I see. . . . Thank you. . . ."

And to Maigret:

"Yesterday morning at about ten. A man with a hoarse voice, or rather one who seemed to have trouble with his breathing. . . ."

Someone who was here for the cure, as Maigret had suspected from the very first, and who, quite by chance, had run into Hélène Lange. No doubt he had discovered where she lived by the simple expedient of following her home. . . .

The telephone rang. It was the inspector whom Lecoeur had dispatched to Lyons. There was no record of the dead woman having stayed in any of the hotels in the town, but he had found a post office clerk who remembered her. She had been in the post office twice, on each occasion to collect a large manilla envelope. The first time, the envelope had lain there a week. On the last occasion, it had just arrived when she called.

"Have you got the dates?"

Thoughtfully, still puffing lingeringly at his pipe, Maigret watched his colleague at work.

"Hello! ... Is that the Crédit Lyonnais?... Have you got out that list of deposits I asked for? ... No.... I'll send for it later today.... Can you tell me if she made deposits on January 14th or 15th, and February 23rd or 24th? ... Yes, I'll hang on."

It didn't take long.

"Eight thousand francs on January 15th, and five thousand on February 23rd of this year...."

"Usually about five thousand francs, you say?"

"Almost always, with a few exceptions. ... I have the figures here. .. I see that, five years ago, the sum of twenty-five thousand francs was credited to her account. ... That's the only time such a large sum was ever paid in."

"In notes, as usual?"

"Yes."

"How does the account stand at the moment?"

"In credit to the tune of four hundred and fifty-two thousand, six hundred and fifty...."

Lecoeur repeated the figure to Maigret.

"She was a rich woman," he murmured, "and still she let furnished rooms during the season...."

The Chief Superintendent's reply surprised him:

"He's a very rich man."

"You're right.... It does look as though she was getting all the money from a single source. A man who can lay out five thousand francs a month, sometimes more ..."

Yet this man had been kept in ignorance of the fact that Hélène Lange was the owner of a little white villa with pale green shutters in the France district of Vichy. Each payment had been made to a different address.

The money had been paid every month, but not any fixed date. Presumably, it was no accident that Mademoiselle Lange had generally allowed a few days to elapse before collecting it, no doubt as a precaution against being seen going into the post office by anyone who might be looking out for her.

A rich man, or at any rate comfortably well off. When he had finally tracked down the sister, he had not attempted to arrange a meeting, but had merely asked her to stay on in Vichy for a day or two, until she heard from him again. . . . Why?

"He must be a married man. . . . Here with his wife, and possibly his children too. . . . Obviously, he's not master of his own time. . . ."

Lecoeur, in his turn, was obviously enjoying seeing Maigret's mind at work. But was it really *his* mind at work? He was making every effort to get inside the mind of the murderer. . . .

"He couldn't find what he was looking for in Rue du Bourbonnais. . . . And he could get nothing out of Hélène Lange. . . . If he had, she would probably still be alive today. . . . He tried to frighten her into telling him whatever it was he wanted to know. . . ."

"Whether his wife is with him or not, we know that he was able to get away that night."

Maigret was silent, pondering this objection.

"What was on at the theater on Monday night?"

Lecoeur took up the receiver to find out.

"*Tosca*. . . . It was sold out."

Moving toward a conclusion, Maigret was not exactly reasoning it out, but rather progressing by leaps of the imagination. Here was this man, a person of some social standing, staying, no doubt, at one of the best hotels in Vichy, with his wife and, very probably, a party of friends.

The night before the performance, or possibly the night before that, he had seen Hélène Lange, and followed her, to find out where she lived.

On the night of the murder, *Tosca* was being performed in the theater of the Grand Casino. Is it not a well-known fact that women are generally more partial than men to Italian grand opera?

"Why don't you go without me? . . . I feel rather tired at the end of the day . . . the treatment . . . I'd be glad of the chance of an early night. . . ."

What was it he wanted to find out from Hélène Lange, which she had so stubbornly refused to tell him?

Had he reached the house before her, forcing the flimsy lock, and searching through drawers and cupboards, while she was still at the concert?

Or had he followed her home, strangled her, and searched the apartment afterward, throwing everything in confusion on the floor?

"What are you smiling at, Chief?

"Something quite absurd that has just occurred to me. . . . Before he had that bit of luck with the

Hôtel de la Gare, the murderer, if he really did telephone all the hotels in alphabetical order, must have made about thirty telephone calls. . . . What does that suggest to you?"

He refilled his pipe, thoughtfully.

"The entire police force is searching for him. . . . Almost certainly he shares a double room in the hotel with his wife. . . . But he's faced with the necessity of repeating the name of his victim aloud, over and over again.

"In a hotel, all phone calls go through the switchboard. . . . Besides, there's his wife. . . . It's reasonable, therefore, to suppose . . .

"Too chancy to make the calls from a café or bar, with the risk of being overheard. . . .

"If I were you, Lecoeur, I should detail as many men as I could spare to watch the public telephone booths."

"But, since he did get through to Francine Lange in the end . . ."

"He'd said he'd call her back. . . ."

"But she's left Vichy. . . ."

"He doesn't know that."

In Paris, Maigret, in common with most married men, saw his wife three times a day, on waking in the morning, at midday, and at night. And often, when he wasn't able to get home for lunch, only twice.

For the rest of the day, for all she knew, he might have been up to anything.

But in Vichy? They, like most other married couples there for the cure, were in each other's company almost twenty-four hours a day.

"He wouldn't have been able to risk a long

absence, even to use a public telephone booth," he said with a sigh.

More than likely he had made some excuse—he was out of cigarettes or wanted a breath of air—while his wife was dressing. . . . One or two quick calls . . . If she too was taking the cure, perhaps having hydrotherapy, that would give him a little more time to himself. . . .

He could imagine him, taking advantage of every opportunity, making opportunities whenever he could, lying to his wife like a naughty child to its mother.

A heavily built man, elderly, rich, of some standing, having come to Vichy in the hope of finding relief from chronic asthma.

"Doesn't it surprise you that the sister has decamped?"

Francine Lange liked money. Heaven knows what depths she had sunk to when she was living in Paris, in order to get it. And now she was the owner of a flourishing business, and her sister's sole heir.

Surely she was not the sort of woman to turn up her nose at the offer of a further substantial sum?

Was it the police she was afraid of? Unlikely, unless she intended to make a clean break, and leave the country.

No! She had gone back to La Rochelle, where she was just as accessible to police questioning as in Vichy. For the moment, she was still on the road with her gigolo at the wheel, in the open, red sports car, which must surely be the envy of every young person who saw it.

For a car like that would eat up the miles. She

would probably reach La Rochelle sometime in the middle of the afternoon.

"Did any of the papers mention that she lived in La Rochelle?"

"No, they just announced her arrival."

"She was a frightened woman already, this morning in the house, and at the cemetery. . . ."

"I wonder why it was you she kept peering at, when she thought we weren't looking. . . ."

"I think I know why. . . ."

Maigret, smiling, went on, though not without some embarrassment:

"I've been built up in the newspapers as a sort of father confessor. . . . She must have been tempted to confide in me, to ask my advice. . . . But then, on reflection, she decided the stakes were too high."

Lecoeur frowned.

"I don't quite see . . ."

"The man tried to get some information out of Hélène Lange. It must have been important, because her refusal to give it drove him berserk. A man doesn't strangle a woman in cold blood. . . . He came unarmed to Rue du Bourbonnais. He never meant to kill her. . . . And then he went away empty-handed. . . ."

Brooding over the manner of her death, Maigret went on:

"If I may venture to say so . . ."

"You mean, he thinks the sister knows what she knew?"

"No doubt about it. . . . Otherwise, he'd never have taken so much trouble and run so many risks to find out where she was staying. . . . He would

128

never have phoned her, and dropped that hint of a large bribe...."

"And what about her? Does she know what he wants from her?"

"It's possible," murmured Maigret, looking at his watch.

"She must, surely? Unless she was scared out of her wits, why should she have run off without a word to us?"

"I must be off to meet my wife...."

He might have added:

"Just like that other fellow!"

Just like that broad-shouldered, corpulent man, who had been forced to resort to every kind of childish trick in order to slip out to a public telephone booth to make his calls.

In the course of their daily walks, the Maigrets might well have passed that particular couple more than once. Who could tell? It was possible that they had sat side by side, drinking their glasses of water, that their chairs . . .

"Don't forget the telephone booths...."

"It would take as many men as you have in Paris...."

"There are never enough.... When will you be calling La Rochelle?"

"About six o'clock, before I leave for Clermont-Ferrand, where I have an appointment with the examining magistrate. I'm seeing him at his house.... This business is worrying him. He's in very well with the Compagnie Fermière, and they don't much care for publicity of this sort.... If you want to be present ..."

He found Madame Maigret waiting for him on

a bench. Never in all their lives had the Maigrets spent so much time sitting on park benches and garden chairs. He was late, but, quick to note that his mood had changed since the morning, she made no mention of it.

How well she knew that preoccupied frown.

"Where are we going?"

"For a walk."

Just as on any other day. Just like the other couple. The wife, surely, could have suspected nothing. How could she guess, as she walked at his side, that he blenched inwardly at the sight of every policeman in uniform?

He was a murderer. He could not cut short his cure and leave, without arousing suspicion. He would have to carry on with the daily round like the Maigrets.

Was he staying at one of the two or three luxury hotels in the town? It wasn't Maigret's business, but if he were in Lecoeur's place . . .

"Lecoeur is a first-class man," he murmured, by which he really meant: "He's sure to think of it. There aren't so many people staying in that class of hotel that . . ."

All the same, he would have liked to ferret about a bit for himself.

"We mustn't forget your appointment with Rian."

"Is it today?"

"No, tomorrow at four. . . ."

He would have to go through it all again, undressing, allowing himself to be prodded and then weighed, listening to the fair-haired young doctor solemnly laying down the law about how many glasses of water he should drink from then on. Perhaps he would prescribe water from one or more of the other springs this time.

He thought of Janvier, who had taken over his office, as Lucas was also away on holiday. He had gone to the mountains, somewhere around Chamonix.

Little boats in single file sailed gently into the wind and, one by one, tacked. Occasionally they saw a couple in a pedal boat. There was a wall all along the Allier, and beyond it, every fifty yards or so, was a miniature golf course.

Maigret caught himself looking back over his shoulder every time they passed a heavily built, elderly man.

To him, Hélène Lange's murderer was no longer a shadowy figure. He was beginning to take shape and assume a personality.

He was somewhere in this town, possibly on one of the promenades where the Maigrets so often walked. He was going through more or less the same motions as themselves, seeing the same sights, the sailing boats, the pedal boats, the yellow chairs in the park, and the constant ebb and flow of the crowds in the streets and gardens.

Rightly or wrongly, Maigret saw him with a woman at his side, perhaps, like himself, rather overweight, complaining of sore feet.

What did they talk about as they walked? What, for that matter, did all the other couples like them talk about?

He had killed Hélène Lange. . . . He was a wanted man. It needed only a careless word or an unguarded action to bring the police about his ears.

A ruined life. His name on the front page of every newspaper. His friends shocked and incredulous. The security of his home and family threatened.

From a luxurious hotel suite to a police cell.

It could all happen in a matter of minutes, or even seconds. At any time, he might feel a strange hand on his shoulder and, turning, see the glint of a police badge.

"You are Monsieur . . . , if I am not mistaken?"

Monsieur what? It was immaterial. His wife's astonished indignation . . .

"It's all a mistake, officer! . . . I know him so well. . . . I should. I'm his wife. . . . Anyone will tell you . . . Say something, Jean!"

Jean or Pierre or Gaston. . . .

Maigret was looking about him blankly, as though he had no idea where he was.

"And even so, he persists . . ."

"What does he persist in?"

"In trying to get at the truth."

"What are you talking about?"

"You know very well whom I'm talking about. . . . He telephoned Francine Lange. . . . He wants to meet her. . . ."

"Surely he won't run the risk of being caught?"

"If only she'd warned Lecoeur in time, he could have set a trap. . . . It's still not too late. . . . He's only heard her voice that once. . . . Lecoeur must have thought of it. . . . One would only need to plant a woman of about her age in Room 406. . . . Then when he rang . . ."

Maigret stopped short where he stood, clenched his fists, and uttered a grunt of fury.

"What the devil can he be at, taking that sort of risk?"

A man's voice answered:

"Hello! Whom do you wish to speak to?"

"Mademoiselle Francine Lange."

"Who is that?"

"Divisional Superintendent Lecoeur."

"Hold on, please."

Maigret was sitting opposite Lecoeur in the bare little office, listening on an extension.

"Hello! Can't it wait till morning?"

"No."

"Can you call back in half an hour?"

"I shall have left by then."

"We've only just got here. . . . Francine, Mademoiselle Lange, that is to say, is in the bath."

"Be good enough to ask her, from me, to get out of it. . . ."

Lecoeur winked at his colleague from Paris. Once again, they heard the voice of Lucien Romanel:

"She won't keep you a moment. She's just rubbing down with a towel. . . ."

"You don't seem to have made very good time. . . ."

"We had a blowout. . . . We wasted an hour trying to get a spare tire. . . . Here she is!"

"Hello!"

Her voice came across more faintly than the gigolo's.

"Mademoiselle Lange? . . . I understood from

133

you this morning that you were planning to spend two or three more days in Vichy. . . ."

"I had intended to, but I changed my mind."

"May I ask why?"

"I could say: 'I just did, that's all.' There's no law against it, is there?"

"No, and there's no law against my taking out a summons to compel you to answer my questions. . . ."

"What difference does it make whether I'm in Vichy or La Rochelle?"

"It makes a great deal of difference to me. . . . I will repeat my question: What made you change your mind?"

"I was frightened. . . ."

"What of?"

"You know the answer to that. . . . I was frightened this morning, but I kept saying to myself that he wouldn't dare . . ."

"Could you be more explicit, please. Whom were you afraid of?"

"Of my sister's murderer. . . . I said to myself, if he attacked her, he's quite capable of attacking me. . . ."

"For what reason?"

"I don't know. . . ."

"Is it someone you know?"

"No. . . ."

"Haven't you the least idea who it could be?"

"No. . . ."

"And yet, having told me that you were staying on in Vichy, you suddenly decided, early this afternoon, that you couldn't get away fast enough. . . ."

"I was frightened. . . ."

"You're lying, or rather prevaricating. . . . You had a very particular reason for being frightened. . . ."

"I told you. . . . He killed my sister. . . . He might equally well . . ."

"For what reason?"

"I don't know. . . ."

"Are you telling me that you don't know why your sister was killed?"

"If I had known, I should have told you. . . ."

"In that case, why didn't you tell me about the phone call?"

He could imagine her wrapped in a bathrobe, with her hair still damp, surrounded by suitcases which she had not yet had time to unpack. Was there an extension in the apartment, he wondered? If not, Romanel must be straining his ears, trying to hear what he was saying.

"What telephone call?"

"The one you received last night at your hotel."

"I don't see what you . . ."

"Do you wish me to repeat what he said? Did he not, in fact, advise you to stay on in Vichy for a day or two longer? Did he not say that he would be getting in touch with you again, and that there could be big money in it for you?"

"I was scarcely listening. . . ."

"Why not?"

"Because I thought it was some sort of spoofing. . . . Isn't that how it struck you?"

"No."

A very emphatic "no," followed by a menacing silence. She was badly shaken, standing there, all those miles away, holding the receiver, and trying to think of something to say.

"I'm not a policeman.... I tell you I thought it was a spoof...."

"Have you ever known it to happen before?"

"Not quite like that...."

"Is it not a fact that you were so badly shaken by this telephone call that you felt you must get away from Vichy as soon as you possibly could?"

"Well, since you obviously don't believe me..."

"If you tell me the truth, I'll believe you...."

"It was frightening...."

"What?"

"The realization that the man was still at large in Vichy.... It's enough to frighten any woman, the thought of a strangler roaming the streets."

"Nevertheless, I haven't noticed any mass exodus from the hotels.... Had you ever heard that voice before?"

"I don't think so...."

"A very distinctive voice...."

"I didn't notice.... I was taken by surprise...."

"Just now you were talking in terms of a spoof...."

"I'm tired.... The day before yesterday I was still on holiday in Majorca. I've scarcely had an hour's sleep since then."

"That's no reason for lying to me."

"I'm not used to being harried in this way. And now you have me out of my bath, and subject me to an inquisition over the telephone...."

"If you wish, I can arrange for my colleague in

La Rochelle to call on you officially in an hour's time, and take down your statement in writing."

"I'm doing my best to answer your questions."

Maigret's eyes sparkled with pleasure. Lecoeur was doing splendidly. He himself would not have set about it in precisely that way, but it would come to the same thing in the end.

"You knew yesterday that the police were looking for your sister's murderer. . . . You must also have known that the smallest clue might prove invaluable. . . ."

"I suppose so, yes."

"Now, there was every reason to believe that your anonymous caller was the murderer. . . . You thought so yourself. . . . In fact, you were sure of it. . . . That's why you were so frightened . . . though I wouldn't have thought you were the type to be easily scared. . . ."

"Maybe I did think it might be the murderer, but I couldn't be sure."

"Anyone else in your place would have informed the police immediately. . . . Why didn't you?"

"Aren't you forgetting that I had just lost my sister—my only relative? . . . She was not even buried. . . ."

"I was at the funeral, remember? You didn't turn a hair."

"What do you know about my feelings?"

"Answer my questions. . . ."

"You might have prevented me from leaving."

"There can't be anything very urgent for you to attend to in La Rochelle, since you were supposed to be still on holiday in Majorca."

"I found the atmosphere oppressive. . . . The thought that that man . . ."

"Or the thought that, if you mentioned the telephone call, you might have to answer some awkward questions?"

"You might have wanted to use me as a decoy. . . . When he called back to suggest a meeting, you might have insisted on my going, and . . ."

"And?"

"Nothing. . . . I was frightened, that's all. . . ."

"Why was your sister murdered?"

"How should I know?"

"Someone whom she hadn't seen for years recognized her, followed her, and forced his way into her house. . . ."

"I thought perhaps she had come upon a burglar unexpectedly. . . ."

"You're not as naïve as all that. . . . There was something he wanted from her, the answer to a question, a vital question. . . ."

"What question?'

"That is precisely what I'm trying to find out. . . . Your sister came into some money, Mademoiselle Lange. . . ."

"From whom?"

"You tell me."

"She and I jointly inherited my mother's estate. . . . She wasn't a rich woman. . . . There was just a little dry goods shop in Marsilly, and a few thousand francs in a savings bank. . . ."

"Was her lover a rich man?"

"What lover?'

"The one who used to call at her apartment in

Rue Notre-Dame-de-Lorette once or twice a week, when she was living in Paris."

"I know nothing about that."

"Did you never meet him?"

"No."

"Don't hang up, mademoiselle, I haven't nearly finished with you yet. . . . Hello!"

"I'm still here. . . ."

"Your sister was a stenographer. . . . You were a manicurist."

"Later I trained as a beautician."

"Quite so. . . . Two young girls from a humble home in Marsilly. . . . You both went to Paris. . . . You didn't go together, but for several years you were both living there at the same time. . . ."

"So what?"

"You claim to know nothing about your sister's life at that time. . . . You can't even tell me where she worked. . . ."

"In the first place, there was a very big difference in our ages. . . . And besides, we never got on, even as children. . . ."

"Let me finish. . . . Not so very long after, you turn up again in La Rochelle—a young woman still—as proprietress of a hairdressing salon, and that must have cost you a pretty penny. . . ."

"I paid a lump sum down, and the rest in yearly installments. . . ."

"We may have to go further into that later. . . . As for your sister, she—if I may put it that way—went out of circulation. . . . To begin with, she moved to Nice, where she spent five years. . . . Did you ever visit her there?"

"No."

"Did you know her address?"

"I got three or four postcards from her. . . ."

"In five years?"

"We had nothing to say to one another."

"And when she came to live in Vichy?"

"She said nothing to me about it."

"You never heard from her that she had moved here permanently, and bought a house?"

"I heard about it from friends."

"Who were these friends?"

"I don't remember. . . . Just some people who had run into her in Vichy. . . ."

"Did they speak to her?"

"They may have. . . . You're confusing me. . . ."

Lecoeur, very pleased with himself, once more winked at Maigret, who was struggling to relight his pipe, which had gone out, without putting down the receiver.

"Did you go to the Crédit Lyonnais?"

"Where?"

"In Vichy."

"No."

"Didn't it occur to you to wonder how much your sister had left you?"

"I shall leave all that to my lawyer here in La Rochelle. I don't understand those things. . . ."

"Indeed? You're a businesswoman, aren't you? Haven't you any idea how much money your sister had in the bank?"

Another long silence.

"I'm waiting. . . ."

"I can't answer that. . . ."

"Why not?"

"Because I don't know. . . ."

"Would it surprise you to learn that it was something approaching five hundred thousand francs?"

"That's a great deal of money."

She sounded rather matter-of-fact about it.

"A lot, I mean, for a girl coming from a little village like Marsilly, who worked as a stenographer in Paris for barely ten years."

"I wasn't in her confidence. . . ."

"Is it not a fact that when you took over the hairdressing business in La Rochelle, it was your sister who provided the money in the first place? Think carefully before you answer, and remember that we have ways and means of getting at the truth."

Another long silence. Between two people who are face to face, silence is less alarming than in the course of a telephone conversation, when all contact is temporarily broken.

"It's surely not a thing you could forget!"

"She did lend me a little money. . . ."

"How much?"

"I'd have to ask my lawyer."

"At that time your sister was still living in Nice, was she not?"

"Possibly. . . . Yes. . . ."

"So you were in touch with her, not just through the exchange of postcards. . . . It seems more than likely that you went to see her, to explain the details of your project. . . ."

"I must have. . . ."

"A moment ago, you denied it."

"All these questions . . . I'm confused. . . . I don't know what I'm saying."

"It's not my questions that are confusing. . . . It's your answers."

"Have you finished with me?"

"Not quite. . . . And I must impress upon you once again that you would be well advised to stay on the line, otherwise I should be forced into taking more drastic measures. . . . This time I want a straight answer, yes or no. . . . In whose name was the deed of sale drawn up, yours or your sister's? In other words, was your sister, in fact, the owner?"

"No."

"Then you were?"

"No."

"Who, then?"

"We owned it jointly."

"In other words, you and she were partners, and yet you've been trying to make me believe that there was no contact between you. . . ."

"It's a family matter, and nobody's business but our own. . . ."

"May I remind you that this is a case of murder?"

"That has nothing to do with it."

"Are you so sure?"

"I hardly think . . ."

"You hardly think . . . In that case why did you rush away from Vichy like a madwoman?"

"Have you any more questions to ask me?"

Maigret nodded, took a pencil from the desk, and scribbled a few words on the pad.

"One moment. . . . Don't hang up. . . ."

"Will you be long?"

"Here it is. . . . You had a child, did you not?"

"I told you so."

"Was it born in Paris?"

"No."

"Why not?"

All Maigret's note said was: "Where was the child born? Where was the birth registered?"

Lecoeur was spinning it out, possibly in order to impress his famous colleague from Paris.

"I didn't want it generally known. . . ."

"Where did you go?"

"Burgundy."

"Where exactly?"

"Mesnil-le-Mont."

"Is that a village?"

"Scarcely more than a hamlet, really."

"Is there a resident doctor?"

"There wasn't then."

"And you chose to have your child in this remote hamlet, out of reach of a doctor?"

"How do you suppose our mothers managed?"

"Was it you who chose the place? Had you been there before?"

"No, I found it on the map."

"Did you go alone?"

"I can't help wondering how you treat criminals, if you can torture innocent people in this way. . . . I haven't done anything. . . . In fact . . ."

"I asked you whether you were alone."

"No."

"That's better. It's much simpler, you know, to tell the truth than to lie. Who went with you?"

"My sister."

"Do you mean your sister Hélène?"

"I have no other."

"This was when you were both living in Paris, and never met except by chance. . . . You had no idea where she worked. . . . For all you knew, she might have been a kept woman. . . ."

"It was no business of mine. . . ."

"You didn't get on. . . . You saw as little as possible of one another, and yet, all of a sudden, she dropped everything, gave up her job, and went with you to some god-forsaken hamlet in Burgundy. . . ."

There was nothing she could say.

"How long were you there?"

"A month."

"In the local hotel?"

"It was just an inn, really."

"Did you have a midwife?"

"I don't know whether she was qualified, but she acted as midwife to all the women in the district."

"What was her name?"

"She was about sixty-five at the time. She must be dead by now."

"Don't you remember her name?"

"Madame Radèche."

"Did you register the birth?"

"Of course."

"You, personally?"

"I was still in bed. . . . My sister went with the innkeeper. He witnessed her signature."

"Did you go yourself later to look at the entry?"

"Why on earth should I?"

"Have you a copy of the birth certificate?"

"It was so long ago . . ."

"Where did you go next?"

144

"Look here, I can't take any more of this. . . . If you must put me through hours of questioning, come and see me here. . . ."

Unmoved, Lecoeur asked:

"Where did you take the child?"

"To Saint-André. Saint-André-du-Lavion, in the Vosges."

"By car?"

"I didn't have a car then. . . ."

"And your sister?"

"She never learned to drive."

"Did she go with you?"

"Yes! Yes! Yes! I'm sick of all this, do you hear me? Sick of it! Sick of it! Sick of it!"

Whereupon she hung up.

6

"What's on your mind?"

In every marriage where husband and wife
have been together for years, each observing the
actions and motions of the other, there are times
when one partner, baffled by the expression on the
other's face, asks diffidently:

"What's on your mind?"

Madame Maigret, it must be said, needed to be
very sure that her husband was not under strain
before she would ask this question, for there were
certain boundaries in their relationship which she
felt she had no right to overstep.

Following the long telephone call to La Rochelle, they had dined quietly in the relaxing atmosphere of the white dining room of their hotel,
with its potted palms in the alcoves, and wine
bottles and flowers on the tables.

Ostensibly, no one paid any attention to the
Maigrets, though they were in fact the focus of
discreet interest, admiration, and affection.

They were now taking their evening walk. From
time to time there was a rumble of thunder in the

sky, and the still evening air was churned up every few minutes by little flurries of wind.

They had come, almost as if by accident, to Rue du Bourbonnais. There was a light showing in one of the upper windows, in the room occupied by the stout widow, Madame Vireveau. The Maleskies were out, walking, possibly, or at the cinema.

On the ground floor, all was darkness and silence. The furniture had been put back in place. Hélène Lange had been blotted out.

Sooner or later, no doubt, the contents of the house would be carted into the street, and the props and chattels which had once been part of a human life would fall under the hammer of some wise-cracking auctioneer.

Had Francine taken away the photographs? It seemed unlikely. Probably she would not even bother to send for them. They, too, would be sold.

They had reached the park where, inevitably it seemed, they always ended up, when Madame Maigret ventured to put her question.

"I'm thinking about Lecoeur. He really is first-class at his job," replied her husband.

The manner in which the Superintendent from Clermont-Ferrand had hammered away at Francine, giving her no time to collect herself, was a good example. He had made the fullest use of the facts at his disposal, to get the fuller information he needed to carry the inquiry a stage further.

Why, then, was Maigret not entirely satisfied? No doubt he would have set about it differently. But then what two men, even when working to the same end, go about it in precisely the same way?

It was not a question of method. Maigret was, if anything, a little envious of his ebullient colleague's assurance and self-confidence.

No, it was something else. To Maigret, the lady in lilac was not just a murder victim. He was not primarily concerned with the kind of life she had led, nor with what had happened to her. He was beginning to know her as an individual and, almost without realizing it, to penetrate the mystery of her personality.

And while he was walking back to his hotel, pondering, to the exclusion of all else, the relationship between the two sisters, Lecoeur was bounding off, without a care in the world, to keep his appointment with the examining magistrate.

What could the examining magistrate really know about a case like this one, closeted in his office, and seeing nothing of life but what was laid before him, encapsulated in the official reports?

Two sisters in a village on the Atlantic coast, a little shop next door to the church. Maigret knew the village, whose people reaped a harvest from both land and sea. A village dominated by four or five big landowners, who were also the owners of oyster beds and mussel farms.

He recalled the women, old women, young women, and little girls, setting out at daybreak, sometimes even at night, depending on the tides, dressed in rubber boots, thick fishermen's jerseys, and shabby men's jackets.

Down on the shore, they gathered the oysters which lay exposed at low tide, while the men scraped the mussels off the wickerwork, which was pegged down by stakes.

Few of these girls were ever educated beyond the most elementary stage, and even the boys fared little better, at least at the time when the Lange girls were growing up.

Hélène was the exception. She had gone to school in the town, and had reached a sufficiently high standard to go to work in an office.

Cycling to work in the morning and returning at night, she was quite the young lady.

And later, her sister too had somehow contrived to better herself.

They are both living in Paris.... They are never to be seen in the village now ... they think themselves too good for us. ...

The girls who had once been their playmates were still going out every morning to gather oysters and mussels. They had married and borne children, who, in their turn, had romped in the square outside the church.

It was cold-blooded determination that had got Hélène Lange what she wanted. Even as a child, she had turned her back on the life that should have been hers. She had mapped out for herself a different life, and retreated into a world of her own, peopled only by the characters in her favorite romantic novels.

She had been unable to stomach Balzac. His world had reminded her too much of Marsilly, her mother's shop, the freezing oyster beds, and the roughened hands of the women.

Francine, too, had managed to escape, in her own fashion. At fifteen, she had had her eyes opened by a taxi driver. She was plump and seductive. Men were attracted by her saucy smile. And why not, she thought, why not turn her charms to good account?

And had she not, in the end, succeeded?

The elder sister had acquired a house in Vichy and amassed a small fortune. The younger had chosen to return home, and flaunt her wealth in the most elegant beauty salon in town.

Lecoeur did not feel the need to enter into their lives, to understand them. He uncovered facts, from which he drew conclusions, and, in consequence, was spared the discomforts of an uneasy conscience.

Intimately concerned with the lives of these two women there was a man. Unidentified, he was nevertheless here in Vichy, in a hotel bedroom, in the park, in one of the gaming rooms of the Grand Casino, somewhere, anywhere.

This man was a killer. And he was caught in a trap. He must know that the police, with their formidable resources, were closing in on him, that the invisible cordon was tightening about him, and that, very soon, the impartial hand of the law would be laid on his shoulder.

He too had a whole life behind him. He had been a child, a youth, he had fallen in love, almost certainly married, or else why should he, the nameless man who had called once or twice a week at Rue Notre-Dame-de-Lorette, not have been able to stay more than an hour at a time?

Hélène had disappeared from Paris. When next heard of, she was living a solitary life in Nice, deliberately shunning attention, it seemed,

150

in that town crowded with people who were all strangers to one another.

Now they knew that, before settling in Nice, she had gone to a tiny village in Burgundy, lived in the local inn for a month, to be with her sister when she gave birth to a child.

Maigret was beginning to understand the two women, but he needed to know more about the man. He was tall and heavily built. He had a distinctive voice, because he suffered from asthma, which was no doubt what had brought him to Vichy in the first place.

He had committed a murder, and gained nothing by it. He had gone to Rue du Bourbonnais, not to take a life, but to ask a question.

Hélène Lange had brought about her own death. She had refused to answer. Even when he had seized her by the throat—probably just to frighten her—she had not spoken, and her silence had cost her her life.

He could have abandoned his quest. It would have been the sensible thing to do. Any further step he took was bound to entail grave risks. The machinery of the law had already been set in motion.

Had he known previously of the existence of the sister, Francine Lange? She claimed that he had not, and she could be telling the truth.

He could have learned from the newspapers that Hélène Lange had a sister, and that she had just arrived in Vichy. He had got it into his head that he must speak to her, and, with astonishing thoroughness and guile, had managed to track her down to her hotel.

Hélène had refused to speak, but would the younger sister prove equally stubborn, if faced with the added inducement of a substantial bribe?

The man was rich, a person of some standing. It must be so, or he could not have afforded to part with more than five hundred thousand francs over a period of a few years.

Five hundred thousand francs in return for what? In return for nothing. He did not even know the address of the woman to whom he sent the money, poste restante, at the various towns designated by her up and down the country.

Had he been able to find her, would Hélène Lange have died sooner?

"Stay on in Vichy for another two or three days. . . ."

It was his last chance. He had to take it, even if it meant getting caught. He would phone her again. It wouldn't be easy, but he would find a way. He would do it as soon as he could escape from his wife without arousing suspicion.

But by now there was scarcely a public telephone booth in the town which was not being watched by one of Lecoeur's men.

Had Maigret been right in believing that he would not risk telephoning from a bar, a café, or his hotel bedroom?

He and his wife walked past one of these public telephone booths. Through the glass panes they could see a teen-age girl chattering away with cheerful animation.

"Do you think he'll be caught?"

"Any time now, yes."

Because here was a man with an overriding obsession. Very likely he had lived with it for years. Probably ever since the very first monthly payment, he had been waiting and hoping for the chance meeting which had occurred at last, after fifteen years.

It might well be that he was a sound business-man, very level-headed as far as his everyday life was concerned.

Fifteen years of brooding . . .

He had squeezed too hard. He never meant to kill her. Or else . . .

Maigret stopped dead in his tracks, right in the middle of a busy boulevard. His wife, with a quick, sidelong glance at his face, stopped too.

"Or else, he came face to face with something so monstrous, so unforeseen, so shocking . . .

"I wonder how Lecoeur will set about it," he murmured.

"Set about what?"

"Getting him to make a clean breast of it. . . ."

"He'll have to find him and arrest him first. . . ."

"He'll give himself up. . . ."

It would be a relief to him to surrender . . . an end to lying and contriving. . . .

"I hope he's not armed."

Because there was a wife in the case, Maigret could envisage an alternative outcome. Instead of giving himself up, the man might decide to end it, once for all. . . .

Had Lecoeur warned his subordinates to proceed with caution? It wasn't for Maigret to interfere. In this instance he was merely a passive spectator, keeping well in the background, as far as was possible.

Even if he did not resist arrest, was there any reason why he should talk? It would not mitigate his crime, nor carry any weight with a jury. To them, he would be just another strangler, and, whatever the provocation, in such a case leniency, still less pity, was not to be hoped for.

"What you really mean is, you wish you were handling it yourself!"

She found that in Vichy she could say things to him that, in Paris, she would never have dared to utter. Was it because they were on holiday?

Because, as a result of being together all day and every day, a new intimacy had grown up between them?

She could almost hear his thoughts.

"I wonder ... No ... I don't think so. ..."

Why should he worry? He was here for a rest, for a thorough clean-out of the system, to use Doctor Rian's phrase. In fact, he had an appointment with the doctor for tomorrow, and then, for half an hour at least, he would be just another patient, preoccupied with his digestion, his liver, his pulse rate, his blood pressure, and his fits of giddiness.

How old was Lecoeur? Barely five years younger than himself. In five years' time, Lecoeur too would be thinking about retirement, and wondering what on earth he would find to do with himself when the time came.

They were behind the casino now, walking past the town's two most luxurious hotels. Long, sleek cars slumbered along the curb. In the garden, to

154

one side of the revolving door, a man in a dinner jacket was leaning back in a deck chair, enjoying the cool of the evening.

A crystal chandelier filled the entrance hall with a blaze of light. They could see oriental carpets, marble pillars, and the liveried hall porter bending forward to answer an inquiry from an old lady in evening dress.

This hotel, or the one next to it, was perhaps where the man was staying. If not, then he was probably at the Pavillon Sévigné, near the Pont Bellerive. Beside the elevator stood a very young page-boy, but not too young to be looking about him with a very supercilious air.

Lecoeur had concentrated his attention on the weakest link, in other words, Francine Lange, and she, taken by surprise, had revealed a good deal.

Presumably he would take the first opportunity of questioning her further. Was there anything more to be got out of her, or had she told all she knew?

"I won't be a minute. . . . I must get some tobacco. . . ."

He went into a noisy bar, where a great many people were looking at a television screen set up on a pedestal above eye level. There was a strong smell of wine and beer. The bald barman was filling glasses without a moment's pause, and a waitress in black dress and white apron was going to and from the tables with laden trays of drinks.

Without thinking, he glanced at the telephone booth, at the far end near the washrooms. It had a glass door. There was no one in it.

"Three ounces of shag."

They were not far from the Hôtel de la Bérézina, and, as they approached, they saw young Dicelle waiting on the steps.

"Could I have a word with you, sir?"

Madame Maigret, leaving them to it, went in to collect her key from the desk.

"Let's walk, shall we?"

Their footsteps echoed in the deserted street.

"Did Lecoeur send you?"

"Yes, he's been on the phone with me. He'd gone home to Clermont, to his wife and kids. . . ."

"How many children has he?"

"Four. The eldest is eighteen. He's shaping up to be a swimming champion. . . ."

"What's been happening?"

"There are ten of us watching the telephone booths. The Super can't spare enough men for all of them, so we're concentrating on those in the center, especially the ones closest to the big hotels."

"Have you made an arrest?"

"Not yet. . . . I'm waiting for the Super. . . . He should be on his way by now. . . . There's been a slip-up, I'm afraid. . . . My fault, entirely. . . . I was on watch near the phone booth in Boulevard Kennedy. . . . It wasn't too difficult to keep out of sight, with all those trees. . . ."

"And you saw a man go in to use the telephone?"

"Yes. . . . A big, heavily built man, answering to the description. He was behaving suspiciously. . . . He kept peering through the door . . . but he didn't see me. . . .

"He began dialing a number, and then, all of a

156

sudden, changed his mind. Maybe I poked my head out too far. I don't know. At any rate, he dialed the first three figures, then thought better of it and came out. . . ."

"And you made no attempt to stop him?"

"My instructions were not to interfere with him in any way, but to follow him. To my surprise, there was a woman waiting for him in the shadows, not twenty yards away. . . ."

"What was she like?"

"Distinguished-looking, well-dressed, fifty-ish. . . ."

"Did you get the impression that there was any collusion between them?"

"No. She just took his arm, and they walked back to the Hôtel des Ambassadeurs."

The hotel with the sumptuous entrance hall and the crystal chandelier, which Maigret had stood and gazed at barely an hour earlier.

"What next?"

"Nothing. The man went up to the desk and got his key from the hall porter, who wished him good night."

"Did you get a good look at him?"

"Enough to know him again. . . . I got the impression that he was older than his wife. . . . Nearer sixty, I'd say. They got into the elevator, and I didn't see them again. . . ."

"Was he wearing a dinner jacket?"

"No, a very well-cut dark suit. . . . He has graying hair brushed back, a healthy complexion, and, I think, a small white mustache. . . ."

"Did you make inquiries at the desk?"

"Of course. He and his wife have a suite—a

large bedroom with an adjoining sitting room—on the first floor, number 105. This is their first visit to Vichy, but they are friends of the proprietor of the hotel, who also owns a hotel in La Baule. The man's name is Louis Pélardeau. He's an industrialist, and lives in Paris, Boulevard Suchet."

"Is he here for the cure?"

"Yes. . . . I asked the hall porter whether he had an unusually distinctive voice. He said yes, he suffered from asthma. . . . They're both being treated by Doctor Rian."

"Is Madame Pélardeau taking the cure as well?"

"Yes. . . . It seems they have no children. . . . They've joined up with some friends from Paris who are staying in the same hotel, and they share a table with them at meals. Occasionally they all go to the theater together."

"Have you got someone watching the hotel?"

"I've put a local man on it, until one of our people gets there, which should be about now. The local fellow, though he had every right to tell me to go to hell, was most co-operative."

Dicelle was obviously thrilled by the whole business.

"He must be the man we're looking for, don't you think?"

Maigret did not answer at once. He lit his pipe with great deliberation. They were less than a hundred yards from the house of the lady in lilac.

"I think he is," he said with a sigh.

The young detective stared at him in amazement. From the way the Chief Superintendent said it, one would really think he regretted it!

158

"I'm to meet my boss outside the hotel. He'll be there in twenty minutes at the outside."

"Did he say whether he wanted me there?"

"He said you'd be sure to come."

"I'll have to let my wife know first."

In the intermission, crowds of people poured out of the Grand Casino theater into the street. Most of the women were wearing sleeveless dresses, cut very low. They and their escorts looked up apprehensively into the sky, which was streaked with intermittent lightning flashes.

Low clouds swirled past, and, worse, to the west the stars were blotted out by a dense, threatening blanket of cloud, moving slowly toward the town.

Outside the Hôtel des Ambassadeurs Maigret and Dicelle waited in silence, watched by the hall porter who, behind his counter of polished wood, stood guard over his nest of pigeonholes and panel of dangling keys.

Just as the first few heavy drops of cold rain were falling, Lecoeur arrived, and, at the same moment, a bell rang, signaling the end of the intermission. It took him some minutes of careful steering and maneuvering to park his car, and when he finally joined them he asked, with a worried frown:

"Is he in his room?"

Dicelle quickly reassured him:

"Number 105 on the first floor. His windows overlook the street. . . ."

"Is his wife with him?"

"Yes. They went up together."

A figure, a uniformed policeman whom Maigret did not recognize, loomed up out of the shadows.

"Am I to stay on watch?" he whispered.

"Yes."

Lecoeur, taking shelter in the doorway, lit a cigarette.

"I am not empowered to make an arrest during the hours between sunset and sunrise, unless a breach of the law is actually committed in my presence."

There was more than a hint of irony in his voice as he cited this section of the Code of Criminal Procedure, adding, thoughtfully:

"What's more, there isn't enough evidence to justify a warrant for his arrest."

It sounded like an appeal to Maigret to help him out of his difficulty, but Maigret did not rise to the bait.

"I don't like leaving him to stew all night. . . . He must have guessed that he's a marked man— why else should he have changed his mind about telephoning?—and I'm puzzled by the presence of his wife, so close to the phone booth." Almost reproachfully, he added:

"What do you say, Chief?"

"I have nothing to say. . . ."

"What would you do, in my place?"

"I shouldn't be inclined to wait, either. . . . I daresay, by now, they're undressing for bed. . . . I should try and avoid going up to their suite. . . . The discreet thing would be to send up a little note."

"Saying what, for instance?"

"That there's someone downstairs who wishes to speak to him on a personal matter. . . ."

"Do you think he'll come?"

"I'm sure of it."

"You'd better wait out here, Dicelle. It wouldn't do for us all to be seen going in together."

Lecoeur went up to the inquiry desk, leaving Maigret standing in the middle of the vast entrance hall, looking about him vaguely. The hall, brilliantly lit by chandeliers, was almost empty, except for an elderly foursome, two men and two women, a long way off—in another world, almost—who were playing bridge. Distance and the deliberateness of their movements made them seem unreal, like characters in a film sequence played in slow motion.

The page-boy, with an envelope in his hand, went briskly up to the elevator.

He heard Lecoeur's voice, muffled:

"Well, we'll soon see . . ."

Then, as though struck by the solemnity of the occasion, he removed his hat. Maigret, too, was bareheaded, holding his straw hat in his hand. Outside, the storm had broken, and the rain was pelting down. They could see a little group of people huddled for shelter on the hotel steps.

In a very short time the page-boy was back.

"Monsieur Pélardeau will be down directly," he announced.

They were both watching the elevator. They could not help themselves. Lecoeur was smoothing his mustache with his forefinger, and Maigret could sense his excitement.

Somewhere up there, a bell was ringing. The

elevator went up, stopped for a moment, and then reappeared.

Out of it stepped a man in a dark suit, with a florid complexion and graying hair. He looked inquiringly around the hall, and then, somewhat hesitantly, came up to the two men.

Lecoeur, who was holding his Superintendent's badge discreetly in the palm of his hand, allowed the man to catch a glimpse of it.

"I should be obliged if I could have a few words with you, Monsieur Pélardeau."

"Now?"

Yes, there was the hoarse voice, just as it had been described to them. The man did not lose his head. There was no doubt that he recognized Maigret, and seemed surprised to find him playing a passive role.

"Yes, now. My car is at the door, if you will be so good as to accompany me to my office."

The florid cheeks turned a shade pale. Pélardeau was a man of about sixty, but his carriage was remarkably upright, and there was great dignity in his bearing and expression.

"I don't suppose it would do any good to refuse."

"None. It would only make matters worse."

A glance at the hall porter, then another at the little far-off alcove, where the four bridge players were still to be seen. A quick look outside at the pouring rain.

"I don't suppose it would be possible for me to get my hat and raincoat from my suite?"

Maigret, meeting Lecoeur's inquiring glance, looked up at the ceiling. It would be cruel, as well as pointless, to leave the wife in suspense up there. It looked like being a long night, and there was little hope of the husband's returning to reassure her.

Lecoeur murmured:

"If you would care to write Madame a note . . . unless she already knows?"

"No. . . . What shall I say?"

"I don't know. . . . That you have been detained longer than you expected?"

The man went up to the desk.

"Can you let me have a sheet of writing paper, Marcel?"

He seemed saddened, rather than shocked or frightened. Using the ball-point pen chained to the desk, he scribbled a few words, declining the envelope that the hall porter held out to him.

"Send this up in five or ten minutes' time, will you?"

"Certainly, sir."

The hall porter looked as though he would have liked to say something more, but, unable to find the right words, merely bowed his head.

"This way."

As Dicelle, by this time sopping wet, opened the rear door, Lecoeur stood by, murmuring instructions in a low voice.

"Get in, please."

The industrialist bent down, and got into the car first.

"You too, Chief."

Maigret, aware that his colleague would not wish their prisoner to be left alone in the back of the car, obeyed. In no time, they were driving through streets crowded with people hurrying for shelter, and huddling together under the trees. There were even people sheltering on the bandstand, under the canopy.

The car turned into the forecourt of the Police Station in Avenue Victoria, and Lecoeur spoke a few words to the officer on duty. There were only one or two lights turned on in the entrance. It seemed a long time to Maigret before they reached Lecoeur's office.

"In here. It's a bit Spartan, but I didn't want to take you all the way to Clermont-Ferrand at this stage."

He removed his hat, but did not venture to take off his jacket, which, like Lecoeur's and Maigret's, was sopping wet about the shoulders. In contrast with the sudden drop in temperature outdoors, the room was very hot and stuffy.

"Take a seat."

Maigret had retreated into his usual corner, and was watching the industrialist, under cover of filling his pipe. The man's face was absolutely impassive, as he looked from one police officer to the other, wondering, no doubt, why Maigret was not playing a more active role.

Lecoeur, playing for time, pulled a memo pad and pencil toward him, and murmured, as though thinking aloud:

"Anything you say at this stage will be off the record. This is not an official interrogation."

The man nodded assent.

"Your name is Louis Pélardeau, and you are an industrialist. You live in Paris, in Boulevard Suchet."

"That's right."

"Married, I take it?"

"Yes."

"Any children?"

After an appreciable pause, he said with an odd note of bitterness:

"No."

"You are here for the cure?"

"Yes."

"Is this your first visit to Vichy?"

"I've passed through it in the car. . . ."

"You've never come here with the specific intention of meeting any particular person?"

"No."

Lecoeur inserted a cigarette into his holder, and lit it. There followed an oppressive silence, then Lecoeur said:

"You know, I presume, why I have brought you here?"

The man, his face still impassive, took time for thought. But Maigret could now see that his blank expression was a sign not of self-control but rather of profound emotional shock.

He was completely numbed, and it was hard to tell whether he realized even where he was, as Lecoeur's voice rang in his ears.

"I would rather not answer that. . . ."

"You came here of your own free will. . . ."

"Yes. . . ."

"You were not unprepared?"

The man turned to Maigret, as though appealing for help, and repeated wearily:

"I would rather not answer that. . . ."

Lecoeur, aware that this was getting him nowhere, doodled on his pad before returning to the attack.

"Soon after your arrival in Vichy, you had an unexpected encounter with someone you had not seen for fifteen years. . . ."

The man's eyes were watering a little, but not with tears. It was perhaps due to the harsh glare of the single naked bulb, which provided all the lighting there was in this bare, usually unoccupied room.

"Was it your intention, when you went out with your wife tonight, to make a telephone call from a public booth?"

After a moment's hesitation, the man nodded.

"In other words, your wife knows nothing?"

"About the telephone call?"

"If you like to put it that way."

"No."

"You mean that there are some matters regarding which she is not in your confidence?"

"You're absolutely right."

"Nevertheless, you did go into a public phone booth. . . ."

"She decided, at the last minute, to come with me. . . . I didn't want to put it off any longer. . . . I told her I'd left the key to our suite in the door, and that I thought I'd better let the hall porter know. . . ."

"Why was it that you didn't even finish dialing the number?"

"I had a feeling I was being watched. . . ."

"Did you see anyone?"

"I saw something move behind a tree. . . . Be-

166

sides, by then I had realized that it was point-less. . . ."

"Why was that?"

He did not answer, but sat motionless, with his hands lying flat on his knees. They were plump, white, well-kept hands.

"Smoke, if you wish."

"I don't smoke."

"You don't mind if I do?"

"My wife smokes a lot . . . far too much. . . ."

"You suspected that the call might be taken by someone other than Francine Lange?"

Once again he did not answer, but neither did he deny it.

"You telephoned her last night, and told her that you would call again to fix an appoint-ment. . . . It's my belief that, when you went into that phone booth this evening, you had already, in your own mind, fixed on a time and place."

"I'm sorry, but I can't help you there. . . ."

He was having difficulty with his breathing, and wheezing slightly as he spoke.

"I assure you, it's not that I want to be obstruc-tive. . . ."

"You would prefer to consult your lawyer first?"

He made a sweeping gesture with his right hand, as though to brush this suggestion aside.

"All the same, you will need a lawyer."

"I'll do whatever the law requires of me."

"You must understand, Monsieur Pélardeau, that, as of now, you are no longer a free man."

Lecoeur showed some delicacy in avoiding the word "arrest," and Maigret was glad of it.

The man had made an impression on both of

them. Here, in this tiny office with its dingy walls, sitting on a rough wooden chair, he seemed larger than life-size, and this impression of stature was enhanced by his astonishingly calm and dignified manner.

Both men had, in their time, questioned many hundreds of suspects. It took a lot to impress them, but this man was truly impressive.

"We could postpone this conversation until tomorrow, but, as I'm sure you'll agree, it would serve no useful purpose."

This, the man seemed to be thinking, was the Superintendent's business, not his.

"What is your particular branch of industry?"

"Steel pressings."

This was a subject on which he could talk freely, and he volunteered one or two particulars, just to show that he was willing to co-operate where he could.

"I inherited a small wire-drawing business near Le Havre from my father. Then gradually I was able to expand and build a plant at Rouen, and another in Strasbourg."

"In other words, you run a very flourishing business?"

"Yes."

He seemed almost to be apologizing for it.

"Your offices are in Paris, I take it?"

"Head office, yes. We have more up-to-date office buildings in Rouen and Strasbourg, but, for sentimental reasons, I've always kept the old head office in Boulevard Voltaire."

It was all past history to him. . . . This evening, in the space of time it took a liveried page-boy to deliver a written message, the greater part of his world had crumbled in ruins.

Probably because he was aware of this, he was willing to talk about it quite freely.

"Have you been married long?"

"Thirty years."

"A woman by the name of Hélène Lange was at one time in your employment, was she not?"

"I'd rather not answer that."

This was his unvarying response, whenever they stepped on dangerous ground.

"You do realize, don't you, Monsieur Pélardeau, that you're making things very difficult for me?"

"I'm sorry."

"If it is your intention to deny the facts which I shall lay before you, I would rather you said so now."

"How can I tell in advance what you are going to say?"

"Are you telling me that you are not guilty?"

"No. . . . In a sense, I am. . . ."

Lecoeur and Maigret exchanged glances. He had made this terrible admission so simply and unaffectedly, without the slightest change of expression.

Maigret was thinking of the park with its great, spreading trees, its expanses of grass which, under the lamp standards, seemed too green to be true, its bandstand and garishly uniformed musicians.

In particular, he was thinking of the long, narrow face of Hélène Lange as he had seen it when, to him and his wife, she was merely the nameless woman they had christened "the lady in lilac."

"Did you know Mademoiselle Lange?"

He sat motionless, gasping as though he were going to choke. It was, in fact, an attack of asthma. He grew purple in the face. He took a handkerchief from his pocket, held it over his open mouth, and was doubled up with a fit of uncontrollable coughing.

Maigret was thankful not to be in his colleague's seat. Let someone else do the dirty work for once.

"I told you . . ."

"Please take your time. . . ."

With eyes streaming, he fought to master the attack of coughing, but it persisted for several minutes.

When at last he straightened up, still red in the face, mopped his forehead and said: "I'm very sorry," the words were scarcely audible.

"I get these attacks several times a day. . . . Doctor Rian tells me that the cure will do me good. . . ."

He seemed suddenly struck with the irony of this remark.

"I should say, would have done me good. . . ."

They shared the same doctor, he and Maigret. Both had undressed in the same gleaming office, both had stretched out on the same couch, over which a white sheet was spread. . . .

"What was it you asked me?"

"Whether you knew Hélène Lange."

"There's no point in denying it."

"You hated her, didn't you?"

If it had been possible, Maigret would have signaled to his colleague that he was on the wrong track.

And indeed the man was staring at Lecoeur in genuine amazement. When, at last, he spoke, this sixty-year-old man sounded as artless as a child.

"Why?" he whispered. "Why should I have hated her?"

He turned to Maigret, as if appealing to him for support.

"Were you in love with her?"

His response was a puzzled frown, which surprised them both. Clearly the last two questions had thrown him off balance and, in some strange sense, changed everything.

"I don't quite see . . ." he stammered.

Then, once more, he looked from one to the other. At Maigret, he looked hard and long.

It was as though they were somehow at cross-purposes.

"You used to go and see her at her apartment in Rue Notre-Dame-de-Lorette."

"Yes," in a tone of voice that implied, "What of it?"

"I presume that it was you who paid her rent?"

He confirmed this with a slight nod.

"Was she your secretary?"

"She was a member of my staff."

"Did your affair with her last long, several years?"

It was obvious that they were still at cross-purposes.

"I used to go and see her once or twice a week. . . ."

"Did your wife know?"

"Obviously not."

"She never found out?"

"Never."

"Doesn't she know, even now?"

The poor man clearly felt that he was beating his head against a brick wall.

"Not even now. . . . All that has nothing to do with . . ."

Nothing to do with what? With the murder? With the telephone calls? They weren't speaking the same language, but neither realized it. No wonder they were baffled by their inability to get across to one another.

7

Lecoeur's glance fell on the telephone on his desk. He seemed about to pick up the receiver when he caught sight of a small white bell-push, and pressed that instead.

"Do you mind? . . . I don't know where this rings, or even if it's working. . . . We'll soon find out at any rate. . . . If anyone comes . . ."

He was playing for time. They waited in silence, avoiding one another's eyes. Of the three men, Pélardeau was probably the most self-possessed, on the surface at least. Admittedly, as far as he was concerned, he had staked his all, and had nothing more to lose.

They heard at last, a long way off, the ringing sound of footsteps on an iron staircase, then on the linoleum of a corridor, drawing nearer, followed by a discreet knock on the door.

"Come in!"

It was a very young, well-scrubbed policeman in uniform. In contrast to the three older men, he fairly radiated youthful vitality.

Lecoeur, who felt something of an interloper in this place, said:

"I wonder if you could spare a moment?"

"Of course, sir. We were just passing the time playing cards."

"We're going out for a moment. Be so good as to stay with Monsieur Pélardeau until we get back."

"It'll be a pleasure, sir."

The young officer, having not the least idea of what it was all about, kept darting puzzled glances at the well-groomed visitor. He could not but be impressed.

A minute or two later, Lecoeur and Maigret were standing in the doorway. The steps leading down to the forecourt were protected by a glass roof, but they could see a glittering curtain of rain in the darkness beyond.

"I was suffocating up there.... I thought you might be glad of a breath of fresh air too."

The heavy storm clouds, streaked from time to time with lightning flashes, were now overhead, and the wind had dropped.

The road was deserted, except for an occasional slow-moving car splashing through the puddles.

The head of the C.I.D. in Clermont-Ferrand, lighting a cigarette, watched the rain beating down on the paved drive, and dripping from the trees in the grounds.

"I know I was making a hash of it, Chief. I ought to have asked you to take over...."

"He was at the end of his tether, numbed with shock. At first, there didn't seem any point in answering your questions. He was determined not to speak, whatever the cost. But, little by little, you won his confidence. What more could I have done?"

"I thought ..."

"You succeeded, up to a point, in breaking down the barriers.... He was beginning to take an interest ... to co-operate even.... Then something went wrong. . . . I don't understand it. It must have been something you said."

"What?"

"I don't know.... All I know is that it switched him off like a light.... I never took my eyes off his face, and at one point I caught a look of absolute astonishment and bewilderment. One would have to go back over every word that was said.... He had been so sure we knew more."

"More about what?"

Maigret sucked at his pipe in silence for a moment.

"Something that to him is patently obvious, but that we have missed. . . ."

"Maybe I should have had someone sitting in, taking a record of the interview. . . ."

"You wouldn't have got a word out of him. . . ."

"Are you sure you wouldn't prefer to take over from here, Chief?"

"Not only would it be irregular, a point which his lawyer might well exploit at a later stage, but I shouldn't handle it any better than you. Quite possibly not so well."

"I honestly don't know where I go from here. The worst of it is that, murderer though he is, I can't help feeling sorry for him.... I'm just not used to handling that sort of man.... He doesn't belong in the realm of crime.... When we came out of the hotel just now, I felt as though he had left a world in ruins behind him. . . ."

"So did he."

"Do you really think so?"

"He refused to play on our sympathy, like a beggar in the streets. . . . He was determined to keep some semblance of dignity, whatever the cost. . . ."

"Will he break down in the end, I wonder?"

"He'll talk."

"Tonight?"

"I shouldn't be surprised."

"Should we carry on here, or . . . ?"

Maigret opened his mouth as though about to speak, then, apparently thinking better of it, closed it again, and relit his pipe. At last he said evasively:

"Don't spring it on him all at once, but you might try leading up to the subject of Mesnil-le-Mont. You could, for instance, ask him if he'd ever been there."

Lecoeur couldn't make out whether he himself attached any great importance to this.

"Do you think the answer will be yes?"

"I couldn't say."

"Why should he have gone there, and what possible bearing could it have on what happened here in Vichy?"

"It was just a thought," replied Maigret apologetically. "When one is adrift, one clutches at straws. . . ."

There was another very young policeman on duty near the entrance, and, in his eyes, the two men standing talking on the stairs were persons of tremendous importance, who had reached the very pinnacle of eminence.

"I wouldn't say no to a glass of beer."

There was a bar on the corner, but there was no

possibility of getting to it in this downpour. As for Maigret, the very word "beer" brought a wry smile to his lips. He had given his word to Rian, and he meant to keep it.

"We'd better go back."

They found the young policeman leaning against the wall. He sprang smartly to attention, and stood motionless, while the prisoner looked from one to the other of the older men.

"Thanks, young man. You can go now."

Lecoeur returned to his seat, and began fidgeting with the memo pad, the pencil, and the telephone.

"I wanted to give you a little time to think, Monsieur Pélardeau. I have no wish to harass you or tie you up in knots. For the present, I'm just feeling my way. . . . One tries to form a general picture, but sometimes one gets hold of the wrong end of the stick. . . ."

He was feeling his way, trying to strike the right note, like a musician tuning up before a concert. The man was watching him closely, but still betrayed no sign of emotion.

"You had been married some time, I take it, when you first met Hélène Lange?"

"I was over forty . . . no longer a young man. . . . I had been married fourteen years. . . ."

"Was it a love match?"

"Love is a word that has different meanings at different stages of a man's life. . . ."

"At any rate, it wasn't a cold-blooded marriage of convenience?"

"No. . . . It was my own free choice. . . . And, in that connection, I have nothing to regret, except the misery I have brought upon my wife. . . . We're

177

very good friends, and always have been. . . . No one could have been more understanding. . . ."

"Even on the subject of Hélène Lange?"

"I never told her. . . ."

"Why not?"

He looked from one to the other.

"It was something I just couldn't talk about. . . . I've never had much to do with women. . . . I've worked hard all my life, and I think perhaps, even in middle age, I was a bit naïve. . . ."

"Was it infatuation?"

"I don't know if that's the right word for it. . . . Hélène was different from anyone I had ever known. . . . I was attracted by her, and yet somehow afraid of her. . . . She was so intense, I didn't know what I was doing. . . ."

"You became lovers?"

"Not at first . . . not for a very long time."

"You mean, she kept you dangling?"

"No, I was reluctant to . . . You see, she had never had a lover. . . . But all this seems very commonplace to you, I daresay. . . . I loved her, or rather, I thought I did. . . . She made no demands; she seemed content to occupy a very small place in my life, just the few hours once or twice a week that you mentioned. . . ."

"Was there ever any question of divorce?"

"Never! Besides, in a different way, I still loved my wife. . . . I would never have agreed to leave her. . . ."

Poor man! He should have stuck to his office, his factories, and his board meetings, where he knew his way about.

"Did she break it off?"

"Yes. . . ."

Lecoeur exchanged a brief look with Maigret.

"Tell me, Monsieur Pélardeau, did you go to Mesnil-le-Mont?"

His face took on an unhealthy, purple flush. With eyes lowered, he stammered:

"No."

"But you knew she was there?"

"Not at the time. . . ."

"Was this after you had parted?"

"She had told me she never wanted to see me again."

"Why was that?"

Once again, that look of utter bewilderment, as though he simply could not make out what was going on.

"She didn't want our child to . . ."

This time, it was Lecoeur whose eyes widened in amazement, while Maigret, apparently not in the least surprised, sat comfortably hunched up, like a contented cat.

"What are you talking about? What child?"

"Why, Hélène's . . . my son. . . ."

In spite of himself, a touch of pride crept into his voice as he spoke of his son.

"Are you telling me that she had a child by you?"

"Yes, my son, Philippe. . . ."

Lecoeur was seething.

"And she hoodwinked you into believing that . . ."

But the man was shaking his head gently.

"There was no question of hoodwinking . . . I have proof."

"What proof?"

"A copy of the birth certificate."

"Signed by the Mayor of Mesnil-le-Mont?"

"Naturally."

"And the woman named as the mother was Hélène Lange?"

"Of course."

"And yet you never went to see this child, whom you believed to be your son?"

"Whom I believe to be my son ... who is my son.... I didn't go because I didn't know where Hélène had hidden herself away to have the child."

"Why all the mystery?"

"Because she was determined that nothing should be done which might, at a later date—how can I put it?—place the child in an equivocal position."

"Wasn't that rather an old-fashioned view to take?"

"You might say so.... But Hélène was old-fashioned in some ways.... She had a strong sense of ..."

"See here, Monsieur Pélardeau, I think I'm beginning to understand, but for the moment, if you don't mind, we'll leave sentiment out of it.... Forgive me for putting it so bluntly, but facts are facts, and there's nothing either of us can do about them...."

"I don't see what you're getting at...."

His outward self-assurance was beginning to give way to a vague uneasiness.

"Did you know Francine Lange?"

"No."

"You never met her in Paris?"

"No. Not in Paris or anywhere else."

"Didn't you know Hélène had a sister?"

180

"Yes. She used to talk of a younger sister. They were orphans. . . . Hélène left college so that her sister . . ."

Unable to contain himself any longer, Lecoeur got to his feet. He remained standing. If there had been room for it, he would have worked off his fury by pacing up and down.

"Go on. . . . Go on. . . ."

He wiped his forehead with the back of his hand.

"So that her sister should have the education she deserved. . . ."

"The education she deserved, indeed! Don't hold it against me, Monsieur Pélardeau, but I'm going to have to cause you a great deal of pain. . . . I ought perhaps to have set about things differently, to have prepared you for the truth. . . ."

"What truth?"

"At fifteen, her sister was a hairdresser's assistant in La Rochelle. She was also, at that time, living with a taxi driver, and he was only the first of heaven knows how many men. . . ."

"She showed me her letters. . . ."

"Whose letters?"

"Francine's. She was at a well-known boarding school in Switzerland."

"Did you actually go there and see for yourself?"

"No, of course not."

"Did you keep her letters?"

"No, I just glanced through them."

"And during the whole of that time, Francine was working as a manicurist in a hairdresser's in the Champs-Elysées! Don't you see, the whole thing, from beginning to end, was a sham?"

The man was still putting up a fight.... But his self-control, though still remarkable, was beginning to crumble, and suddenly his mouth twisted in an expression so pitiable that Maigret and Lecoeur could not bear to look at him.

"It's not possible," he stammered.

"Regrettably, it's the truth."

"But why?"

It was a last desperate bid to avert his fate. Let them say right out, here and now that it wasn't true, that it was an ignoble police trick to undermine his resistance.

"I'm sorry, Monsieur Pélardeau. Until tonight, up to this very minute, I too never suspected the extent to which those two were in collusion."

He started to lower himself into his chair, but then sprang up again. He was still too overwrought to sit down.

"Did Hélène never raise the subject of marriage?"

"No...."

This time, he sounded less confident.

"Even when she told you she was pregnant?"

"She didn't want to break up my home...."

"In other words, you did discuss marriage...."

"Not in the way you mean.... Only to explain why she was proposing to disappear...."

"To commit suicide?"

"There was never any question of that.... But as the child would not be legitimate ..."

Lecoeur sighed and, once more, exchanged glances with Maigret. Each knew what the other was thinking. Both, in imagination, were dwelling

182

on the exchanges that must have taken place between Hélène Lange and her lover.

"You don't believe me. . . . I myself . . ."

"You must try and face up to the truth. . . . Self-deception won't help you now. . . ."

"Can anything help me now?"

With a sweeping gesture, he indicated the walls of the little office, as though, to him, they were the walls of a prison cell.

"Let me finish. . . . I know it will sound mawkish to you, but she wanted to devote the rest of her life to bringing up our child, in the same way as she had brought up her sister."

"And you were not to be allowed to see your child?"

"On what terms? How could she explain me to him?"

"You might have been an uncle . . . a friend. . . ."

"Hélène hated lying. . . ."

His voice had suddenly taken on a faintly ironic inflection. It was a hopeful sign.

"So she was determined that your son should never know that you were his father?"

"Later, when he came of age, she was going to tell him. . . ."

He added, in his strange, hoarse voice:

"He's fifteen now. . . ."

Lecoeur and Maigret listened in painful silence.

"When I saw her in Vichy, I decided . . ."

"Go on."

"That I must see him, or at least find out where he was. . . ."

"And did you?"

He shook his head, and this time there were real tears in his eyes.

"No."

"Did Hélène tell you where she was going to have the child?"

"In a village she knew. . . . She didn't tell me the name. . . . Then, two months later, she sent me a copy of the birth certificate. The letter was posted in Marseilles. . . ."

"How much money did you give her before she left?"

"Does it matter?"

"It matters a great deal, as you will see."

"Twenty thousand francs. . . . I sent thirty thousand more to her in Marseilles. . . . Naturally, it was my wish that, thereafter, she should have a regular allowance, to enable her to give our son the best of everything. . . ."

"Five thousand francs a month?"

"Yes. . . ."

"What reason did she give for wanting the money to be sent to a different town each time . . . ?"

"She was afraid I wouldn't have the will power . . ."

"Was that what she said?"

"Yes. . . . I had agreed, in the end, not to see the child until he came of age. . . ."

Lecoeur's look plainly asked Maigret:

"What's to be done?"

But Maigret only blinked rapidly two or three times, and bit hard on the stem of his pipe.

8

Lecoeur was sitting down, having lowered himself very slowly into his seat. He turned to the man whose puckered face revealed all that he had just had to endure, and said, almost sorrowfully:

"I'm going to have to cause you still more pain, Monsieur Pélardeau."

The man responded with an embittered smile, as though to say:

"Is that possible, do you think?"

"I feel for you, and indeed respect you as a man. . . . I'm not fabricating all this to trick you into making admissions which, anyway, would be superfluous. . . . What I have to tell you now, like everything I have told you so far, is strictly true, and no one is more sorry than I am that the truth should be so harsh. . . ."

A pause, to give his hearer time to prepare himself.

"You never had a son by Hélène Lange."

He had expected a vehement denial, or at least a violent outburst of some sort, but he was met with a blank, expressionless stare, and silence. This was a broken man.

"Did you never have any suspicion?"

Pélardeau raised his head, shook it, and put his hand to his throat to indicate that, for the moment, he was unable to speak. He barely had time to get his handkerchief out of his pocket when he was racked by another attack of asthma, more violent than the first.

In the silence that followed, Maigret became aware that outside too it had grown silent. The thunder had ceased, and the rain was no longer thudding down.

"I'm sorry. . . ."

"You did have occasion to suspect the truth, didn't you?"

"Once. . . . Only once."

"When?"

"Here . . . that night. . . ."

"When did you first see her?"

"Two days before. . . ."

"Did you follow her?"

"Yes, keeping out of sight . . . to find out where she lived. I was waiting for her to come out with my son, or to see him come out alone. . . ."

"On Monday night, did you speak to her as she was going into the house?"

"No. . . . I saw the lodgers go out. . . . I knew she was in the park, listening to the music. . . . She always liked music. . . . I had no difficulty in opening the door. . . . The key of my hotel room fitted the lock. . . ."

"You searched through the drawers?"

"The first thing I noticed was that there was only a single bed. . . ."

"What about the photographs?"

"They were all of her. . . . Not one of anyone

else. . . . I would have given anything to have found a photograph of a child. . . ."

"And letters?"

"Yes. . . . I couldn't understand it. . . . There was nothing. Even if Philippe was away at boarding school, he must have . . ."

"And she found you there when she got in?"

"Yes. I begged her to tell me where our son was. . . . I remember asking her if he was dead . . . if there had been an accident."

"And she wouldn't answer?"

"She took it all much more calmly than I did. She reminded me of our pact."

"That she would give you your son when he reached the age of twenty-one?"

"Yes. . . . On condition that I should never make any attempt to see him before then."

"Did she talk about him?"

"In great detail. . . . About when he cut his first teeth. . . . His childhood ailments. . . . The nurse she engaged to look after him when she herself was unwell. . . . Then school. . . . She gave me almost a day-by-day account of his life."

"But she never said where he was?"

"No. . . . She said that recently he had begun to take a great interest in medicine . . . that he wanted to become a doctor. . . ."

He looked straight at the Superintendent, without embarrassment.

"There was no such boy?"

"Yes, there was. . . . But he was not your son. . . ."

"You mean there was another man?"

Lecoeur shook his head.

"It was Francine Lange who gave birth to a son

187

at Mesnil-le-Mont.... I confess that, until you told me so yourself, I had no idea that Hélène Lange had registered the child as her own.... The plan must have occurred to the sisters when Francine Lange found she was pregnant.... If I know anything about Francine, her first thought must have been to get rid of it.... Her sister was more far-sighted...."

"It came to me in a flash, as I told you.... That night, when I found that she was deaf to my entreaties, I used threats.... For fifteen years I had looked forward with longing to the time when I should see this son of mine. My wife and I have no children of our own.... When I knew that I was a father ... But what's the use?"

"You took her by the throat?"

"To frighten her, to make her talk.... I shouted at her.... I demanded the truth.... I never thought of the sister ... but I feared that the child was dead, or crippled...."

His hands slipped out of his lap and hung down limply, as though all the strength of that great, burly frame had drained away.

"I squeezed too hard.... I didn't realize.... If only she had shown the faintest spark of feeling! But she didn't ... not even of fear...."

"When you read in the paper that her sister was in Vichy, it gave you fresh hope?"

"If the child was alive and Hélène was the only person who knew where he was, there was no one left to care for him.... I knew I must expect to be arrested at any time.... You must have found my fingerprints."

"Without knowing whose they were ... though,

in the end, we would have caught up with you. . . ."

"I had to know, to make provision. . . ."

"You worked your way in alphabetical order, through the list of hotels. . . ."

"How did you know?"

It was childish, but Lecoeur badly felt the need of a boost to his self-esteem.

"Each time you used a different phone booth."

"So you had tracked me down already?"

"Almost."

"But what about Philippe?"

"Francine Lange's son was put out to foster parents soon after birth—a family called Berteaux, small tenant farmers at Saint-André-du-Lavion, in the Vosges. . . . The sisters used your money to buy a hairdressing salon in La Rochelle. . . . Neither of them took the slightest interest in the child. . . . He lived with his foster parents in the country until, at the age of two and a half, he was drowned in a pond."

"He's dead, then?"

"Yes. . . . But, as far as you were concerned, he had to be kept alive. All that about his childhood, his early schooling, his pranks, and his recent interest in medicine, was made up on the spur of the moment."

"How monstrous!"

"Yes."

"To think that any woman could . . ."

He shook his head.

"It's not that I don't believe you . . . but, somehow, my whole being revolts. . . ."

"It's not the first case of its kind in the history of crime. . . . I could tell you of others. . . ."

"No," he begged.

He sat hunched up, limp. There was nothing left for him to cling to.

"You were quite right, just now, when you said that you didn't need a lawyer. . . . You have only to tell your story to a jury. . . ."

He put his head in his hands and sat there, very still.

"Your wife must be getting anxious. . . . In my opinion, it would be kinder to tell her the truth—otherwise she'll be imagining much worse things. . . ."

He raised a flushed face to Lecoeur. He had probably forgotten her until then.

"What am I going to say to her?"

"Unfortunately, for the present, you won't have an opportunity to say anything to her. . . . I am not at liberty to release you, even for a very short time . . . You will have to accompany me to Clermont-Ferrand. But, unless the examining magistrate objects, which I'm certain he won't, your wife will be able to visit you there."

Pélardeau, deeply disturbed on his wife's account, turned, in desperation, to Maigret:

"Couldn't you see to it?"

Maigret looked inquiringly at Lecoeur, who shrugged as if to say that it was no concern of his.

"I'll do my best."

"You'll have to be careful, because my wife has suffered from a weak heart for some years. . . . We're neither of us young any more. . . ."

Nor was Maigret. Tonight, he felt old. He couldn't wait to get back to his wife, and resume the humdrum routine of their daily life, walking through the streets of Vichy, sitting on the little yellow chairs in the park.

They went downstairs together.

"Do you want a lift, Chief?"

"I'd rather walk."

The streets were glistening. The black car, taking Lecoeur and Pélardeau to Clermont-Ferrand, disappeared in the distance.

Maigret lit his pipe and, without thinking, put his hands in his pockets. It wasn't cold, but the temperature had dropped several degrees after the storm.

The shrubs on either side of the entrance to the Hôtel de la Bérézina were dripping.

"Here you are at last!" exclaimed Madame Maigret, getting out of bed to welcome him. "I dreamed you were at the Quai des Orfèvres questioning a suspect, and having beer sent up to you every five minutes. . . ."

But when she had had time to take a good look at him, her voice changed, and she murmured:

"It's over, then?"

"Yes."

"Who did it?"

"A very respectable man. Had charge of thousands of office and factory workers, but he never learned much about the ways of the world."

"I hope you'll be able to sleep late tomorrow morning."

"I'm afraid not. . . . I've got to go and explain to his wife. . . ."

"Doesn't she know?"

"No."

"Is she here in Vichy?"

"At the Hôtel des Ambassadeurs."

"What about him?"

"Within the next half-hour he'll be behind bars in the Clermont-Ferrand prison."

She watched him closely as he undressed, but could not quite interpret his rather odd expression.

"How many years do you think he'll . . ."

Maigret always liked to have two or three puffs at his pipe before going to bed. He was filling it now. Without looking up, he said:

"He'll be acquitted, I hope."

Epalinges, September 11, 1967